Crossed signals . . .

"Well, Mr. High and Mighty, despite what others have said, even I didn't think you were low enough to make me an *indecent* proposal."

"Come now, Belle," he reasoned. "You know I could not propose marriage. I owe my family and my name more than that."

Her blue eyes glimmered in fury. "And what about my honor?" she cried. "I do come from a good family, and I have never done anything that would make them ashamed of me, like offering *carte blanche* to a gently reared female, my lord." Cristabel took a deep breath and continued: "Futhermore, I would never, no matter how dire my circumstances, accept cupboard kisses from a man who would hide me away in a little love nest somewhere while he danced at all the grand balls with 'eligible' females and even married one. You, sir, are a rake and a libertine. I pray I never see you again!"

Cupboard
Kisses

Barbara Metzger

A SIGNET BOOK

SIGNET
Published by New American Library, a division of
Penguin Putnam Inc., 375 Hudson Street,
New York, New York 10014, U.S.A.
Penguin Books Ltd, 27 Wrights Lane,
London W8 5TZ, England
Penguin Books Australia Ltd,
Ringwood, Victoria, Australia
Penguin Books Canada Ltd, 10 Alcorn Avenue,
Toronto, Ontario, Canada M4V 3B2
Penguin Books (N.Z.) Ltd, 182–190 Wairau Road,
Auckland 10, New Zealand

Penguin Books Ltd, Registered Offices:
Harmondsworth, Middlesex, England

Published by Signet, an imprint of New American Library,
a division of Penguin Putnam Inc.
Previously published in a Fawcett paperback edition.

First Printing (Fawcett), December 1989
First Signet Printing, January 2001
10 9 8 7 6 5 4 3 2 1

This one's for Gail and Noisy,
for their love and loyalty

Chapter One

"**D**ash it, Kenley, it's two in the morning and you're in no condition to make a night of it. Let's go on home."

"You're wrong, my friend. Home is precisely where I'm in no condition to be. Much too sober. One more club ought to do the trick."

The two gentlemen were standing on the empty pavement outside Brooks's, one of London's exclusive men's clubs. The shorter of the two looked up and down St. James's Street, where a few sporadic street lamps lit the way.

"You've already sampled the brandy of every respectable place. Where would you like to continue the exercise?"

"Why, an unrespectable one, of course! You're the London expert though, Perry, the compleat town buck. You lead on."

"There's Hazlip's a few blocks away," Perry answered, knowing it was hopeless to protest further. "Shall I call for my carriage?"

"For two blocks? Gads, man, stop fussing. Since when did you turn into a nursemaid anyway?"

"Since you forgot to duck, damn you, Chase! You've been wounded, near drowned, gaoled in a French warship's brig till you almost died from the gunshot in your brain box, and now—"

"And now I am going to enjoy myself," firmly declared Captain Kenley Chase, late of His Majesty's warship *Invicta,* which was presently lying at the bottom of the sea. "I'll grant you I am not ready for total debauchery," he said, gesturing to his forehead, where the dim light barely showed the edges of the black eye patch he wore. "Women seem to prefer dueling scars, you know. But some heady wine, heavy wagers, and good fellowship are just what I needed, especially tonight."

Perry cleared his throat, choking on the concern he'd almost displayed, obviously unwelcome to his companion and contrary to his own habitual Corinthian attitude of weary boredom. The two men had been friends since Eton, though, no matter how far apart their paths had wandered, and the emotion was there. Perry disguised it with a reminder that Chase had visited Hazlip's on his last leave, nearly two years ago.

"The place ain't White's, of course, but the wine isn't watered, and the dice aren't weighted, and, well, I'll stand by to carry you into the carriage for the ride home."

The captain put his arm around the smaller man and chuckled. "You and how many footmen, bantling?" He squeezed Perry's shoulder in silent appreciation as the two men walked down the nearly deserted street.

Chase's slightly rolling gait, legs spread as if to maintain balance, was what one could expect from a man used to maneuvering on a pitching deck. Almost fifteen years at sea had left at least that mark on him. Otherwise the two comrades could have been any ordinary Regency gentlemen, slightly on the go, out for an evening's amusement. It wasn't till they reached the lamp's glow in Hazlip's entryway that the real differences showed between Kenley Chase and his friend Perry Adler, nay, between the naval veteran and most other gentlemen in the top ranks of London society.

Perry handed over his greatcoat, with ten capes at least, his gloves, his ornamental walking stick, and high hat, distributing smiles and gratuities alike with easy charm. His dress was totally à la mode, from his black coat and waist, to gleaming white starched cravat, to the one precise fob chain dangling at his somewhat stocky waist. He had thinning blond hair attempting a Brutus cut and a rounded face that kept him still boyish-looking at thirty-two, especially when he smiled, which he did now at Hazlip's effusive greeting.

"Welcome, welcome, Mr. Adler. We've missed you. How are you on this fine night? It's always a pleasure to see you young gentlemen here. Not like some, who don't know their limits, heh heh." The proprietor glanced worriedly at the back of Mr. Adler's large, dark-haired companion, now struggling to extricate himself from his greatcoat. Not another foxed, belligerent nob, Hazlip prayed to himself. At least not the new chandelier, please Lord. Ah, he sighed in relief, recognizing the man who finally turned his way.

"Why, it's Captain Chase, isn't it? What a happy surprise! Sir, may I tell you how honored we are to have you visit Hazlip's, and what a fine pleasure, yes, pleasure indeed, to see you back from the war alive and we . . . we . . . Welcome, Captain."

Chase inclined his head the barest fraction in acknowledgment. He'd gotten rid of his greatcoat, which was serviceable, no capes, and handed over his gloves. He had no hat, no cane, and no smile for the bumbling toadeater. What he had was his dress uniform, adorned with gold braid and hanging loosely on his tall frame everywhere but at his broad shoulders. He had dark, curly hair, not combed into a Windswept or anything purposeful, simply allowed to fall forward over his forehead. He had a lined, weathered face from his career at sea, but instead of the swarthy complexion one might have expected from those years of exposure, his face wore an ashen pallor, making him look years older than Perry when, at thirty-one, Kenley was actually the younger man. The eye patch didn't help, except that it covered most of an angry red gash that ran jaggedly up his forehead until lost in the forward-falling curls. His other eye was gray where it wasn't bloodshot. The look he gave the proprietor, turning his head to do so, was glassy-eyed and cold. No one, not even an avaricious nodcock like the gaming hall owner, could have said he looked well.

"Clunch," he muttered under his breath as he and Perry moved into the gaming rooms proper.

"I warned you this place mightn't be up to snuff, Lee," Perry reminded, helping himself to a glass from a passing waiter. He handed another to Chase.

The captain sipped some of the ruby liquid and grimaced.

"What, has it turned? We've had so blasted much to drink tonight I wouldn't think you could tell Bohea from blue ruin."

"No, no, the wine is excellent. French, unmistakably, and almost as certainly not under a revenuer's label. Damn, how those dastards slip through the blockade!"

"You cannot be against a little free trading, can you? It's . . . it's the British way."

"Nay, I'd not gainsay the *ton* its wines and laces or

even the poor fisherman trying to make an easier living. It's the gold that goes *back* to France that galls me. All that money, right into Bonaparte's coffers, buying guns, horses, and soldiers' loyalties."

"Do you wish to leave, then?" Perry asked anxiously. "Doesn't sound like you'd enjoy yourself here. I know I've got some cognac m'father put down years ago. No need to worry for the excise."

Chase smiled, a not-quite-cheerful look on his haggard face. "What a trial I am to you. I don't mean to be such a bear. No, this is exactly what I wanted, the British way and all." He took a deep breath. "Just smell that, stale smoke and spilled wine, unwashed bodies and yes, the delicate bouquet of mildew. Now I know I'm home in England!"

"Gammon. Next you'll be wanting a welcome back party in the stews at Seven Dials." Adler waved his arms around the room. "So what's your pleasure? Dice? Hazard? That's young Torrington playing vingt-et-un in the corner. It's bellows to mend with him, vowels all over town. The old earl suddenly refused to make good on them, they say. Too late if you ask me."

They were strolling around slowly, Adler nodding to acquaintances, making a few introductions to those men not rapt in their wagering. Chase stopped him with a hand on his sleeve. "Perry, am I seeing things, or does the faro dealer have pointed teeth?" The room was so blanketed in concentration even his whisper sounded loud in the hush.

An older man at the nearest table glanced up from his cards and explained, "It's all the rage now. The young jackanapes file their front teeth down, supposedly so they can spit through 'em, like coachmen." He laughed at the captain's shudder. "It's nothing compared to when they think they can *drive* like coachmen. The name's Rampling, by the way. Care for a hand or two of whist?"

Perry was still trying to focus his monocle on the faro dealer. "Damn if you can't see better with one eye than I can with two and my quizzing glass. Anyway, I don't know where chaps get these gnaggy notions," he said as he sat down next to Rampling, who was wearing his jacket inside out—to change his luck.

The jacket reversed again, and Rampling's losing streak still held. He tossed in his last hand. "That's it for me, sir. I thought you'd be less attentive to the cards. My mistake."

Adler lightened another waiter's load and grinned at the older man. "What, the eye patch?" he teased. "That's just to make him look interesting, don't you know. Give him a week on the town and you'll see all the young fops sporting 'em."

"Satin, I'd bet, in colors to match their waistcoats."

Perry disagreed. "I'd put my money on black, more gothic, romantic."

Chase, meantime, impatiently drummed his fingers on the table. He got up and wandered off when the other two got down to the particulars of an actual bet. On eye patches, by Jove!

An old debauchee now held the bank at the faro table. He called the captain over to try his luck at a real man's game, not one of those chicken-stakes drawing room pastimes. Chase recognized the speaker as Baron Harwood, a dissolute gambler who'd been frequenting the gaming halls since before Chase went into the Navy. Harwood had pouches under his eyes, yellowed teeth, food stains on his linen, and wore his hair slicked back with greasy pomatum. The captain didn't want to sit at the same table, much less play with such a loose screw. He declined with a slight shake of his head.

"What's the matter, hm, fortune at low tide, Captain?" Harwood quipped. "Or maybe I should say 'my lord.' It's Viscount Winstoke now, ain't it? Damn if the young gudgeon don't go off to war all hot to hand, comes back a hero, and walks into a title and handsome fortune at the same time. Blast if I want to play with such a lucky devil, after all."

Lucky, when he'd lost his ship and perhaps his eyesight? Lucky to come into a title by losing a well-loved brother? He'd show that miserable maw-worm a thing or two about luck!

"Captain will do, until I resign my commission, my lord," Chase replied into the quiet following Harwood's drunken mutterings. He clenched his teeth and sat down, taking the farthest seat from the baron possible. He gestured for another glass and a fresh deck of cards. Softly, during the wait, he asked, "I wonder how pleased you would be to hear your heir calling himself the most fortunate of fellows."

Harwood cackled. "No one's taking post-obits out on me, boy. Got no hopefuls waiting for the title at all. Just a plaguey old-maid schoolmarm of a niece somewhere. M'brother got religion before he died so the blasted female thought she could preach to me about my duties. Hah! No dragon in Puritan petticoats is telling Charles Harwood how to spend the ready. Are we going to play, *Captain*, or are you saving your blunt for your grandchildren?"

They played. The only sounds were the slap of cards, the rustle and clink of bets being laid down and then swept to one pile or another. Harwood's pile dwindled. Chase's grew. Drinks were forgotten, leaving wet marks on the table; new candles were lit as old ones added their guttering smoke to the room's haze. Soon Harwood and the captain were the only players in the game, drawing spectators from the other tables.

Harwood lost another round and there were no more notes, coins, or chips in front of him. Perry Adler, standing behind his friend's chair, let out a sigh of relief. Good, now they could go home. All the watchers turned to Harwood, who was staring at the captain, weighing his chances. Kenley was squeezing the bridge of his nose with a shaking hand; sweat beaded on his forehead. The wound above his eye looked raw, inflamed.

"Will you accept my marker?" Harwood had decided. "It's good, I assure you."

Chase looked behind him to Perry, as if to ask if the bet would be honored, but it was Rampling, catching the glance, who nodded in the affirmative. Perry groaned when his friend called Hazlip himself over to bring paper and pen.

Harwood gave a last calculating look in Chase's direction before dipping the pen. "Bloody fool can't last much longer," he groused, figuring the captain's luck—or concentration—would have to desert him soon. The baron tossed his note onto the center of the table.

"Long enough for this," Chase answered, bringing an angry flush to the older man's already whiskey-florid face. Those few men around the table who may have thought about joining the game thought again when they caught the captain's one-eyed glare. Hazlip stayed nearby with the pen and ink.

Harwood pondered every discard. Chase fumbled for a handkerchief to wipe his moist forehead, tossing down a seemingly random selection. Yet now a flurry of white scraps joined the stacks in front of him. While Harwood wrote, Chase neatened the piles. One for coins and chips, one for bank notes, and one, growing steadily, for Harwood's vouchers.

Beads of perspiration dripped onto the table, a trembling hand sloshed liquor onto a lace-edged cuff—and Kenley Chase wasn't feeling too well either.

Finally, finally he stood to leave, holding onto the chair back. "Get that, will you, old man?" he asked Perry, gesturing to his winnings.

"One more hand, Captain. Just one more hand," the baron whined, almost begging. "I know my luck will turn. You can't leave now. You're winning, blast you."

"Oh, yes you can," Adler exploded, all his frustrated anxieties finally bursting forth. "You've been winning all night, and you'll go on winning as long as this bedlamite has something to lose—and look at you! You can barely stand, you can hardly hold the cards! Blister it, you should be home in bed. Did you forget about the surgery tomorrow?"

Chase sat down again, heavily. "I was trying to, Perry, by God I was. Almost did it, too. I need a drink."

Almost. It was hard to forget when his head ached and his vision blurred. It was hard to forget when the best physicians the Admiralty could find all agreed he'd certainly die without the operation to remove the metal shard lodged above his eye. Brain fever, they'd said. Putrefaction, they'd said. Of course, they'd also said that he could be blind in both eyes after the operation—if he lived through it. What were the odds? he'd pleaded to know. One doctor just shook his head; another tried to be conciliatory: Just hope for the best, he'd soothed, before a calloused fist smashed down on his desk, making the inkwell bounce.

"By Jupiter, man, this isn't a horse race," the harried physician finally declared. "But you won't even make it to the starting line without the surgery. With it, at least you're in the running. I'm sorry, lad, but all of life is a gamble."

The war hero turned back to the aged, dissipated nobleman. "Do you have anything left to lose, my lord?"

"My London property," Harwood bleated, scribbling furiously. "It's worth plenty. No heir, no entailment. It'll bring me luck, I know it will."

It didn't.

Some forty-five minutes later Captain Chase stood up again. He looked across the table at his opponent, who was staring vacantly ahead through red-rimmed, damp eyes, a string of drool trailing from his open mouth. "Take me home, Perry. I find I don't wish this"—the smoke and stains, the raddled nobility—"to be my last sight of England after all."

"I do wish I'd gotten to go home first, seen my mother." The two friends were at last at Perry's bachelor rooms at the Albany, Chase's temporary "home," but Adler understood.

"Staffordshire's too far," he told Chase, "and the roads are in deplorable condition this time of year, in the middle of the thaws. You'll get there soon."

"Perhaps, perhaps," the captain answered.

They were relaxed in worn old leather armchairs near the fire, waiting for dawn. Kenley held a glass; Perry'd stopped drinking hours ago, lest his sick friend have to tend to *him*. He couldn't understand what was keeping Chase awake, much less alert, unless it was his unpleasant thoughts.

"Do you know how many times I've faced death?" Chase asked, more to himself than to Perry, who merely went "hmm." Chase rambled on: "I'd rather face a hundred battles than this . . . this . . ."

"Not to worry, you'll be back at the helm of some warship soon enough. The Admiralty couldn't get on without you hero types."

"No, I've decided to sell out, either way." Kenley snorted. "Can you imagine a blind sea captain? If, on the other hand, things go well, I'll have to take my brother's place in Staffordshire, for all that I know about husbandry. It's amazing how fate gets so quirky, isn't is? My brother was born to the land. He knew every inch of that estate and all the tenants. I swear he knew the name of every pig. And *he* drowns in a sailing accident. On a blasted lake!"

Chase reached over to the cluttered table between them to refill his glass. His eye caught the mound of currency and notes scattered there.

"All of my, ah, affairs are in order, Perry, but if anything . . . you know. You keep this. Send the property back to that old curmudgeon, but keep the money."

"Dash it, man, I don't need your blunt."

"Of course you don't, but old Harwood would only gamble it away again anyway. Have a party. Yes, I'd like that. A bright, noisy party with champagne and pretty girls." Chase reached for the decanter again. After he'd filled his glass, he picked up another bottle, but this one was mounted on its side, with a replica of the ship *Invicta* encased within. "At least I won't face this day sober," he said, as the glass slipped from his limp fingers to the floor. The ship-in-a-bottle, however, stayed tenderly cradled in his lap.

Charles Swann, Baron Harwood, went home, too. He closeted himself in his library with his books, bills, and bank statements. Then he blew his brains out, choosing not to face the coming day at all.

Chapter Two

Miss Meadow believed in treating the young ladies at her select academy with all the care and consideration due their ranks and future social standings. She also, unfortunately, believed in treating the instructors at her fashionable boarding school according to the same standards. This evening, for example, Miss Meadow entertained three of the upper-class students for coffee and dessert in her office/sitting room, designed to accustom them to the polite world they would soon be joining. Correspondingly, Miss Cristabel Swann, the music teacher, sat demurely outside Miss Meadow's office in the hard chair reserved for those girls awaiting one of the headmistress's mottoes and precepts lectures.

One of Miss Meadow's favorite moral lessons was Moderation. She constantly reminded her young ladies not of Aristotle, but to think small: small steps, small bites, small displays of emotion. A little spirit was acceptable, lest the girls be considered milk-and-water misses. Any wider displays of feeling, loud laughter, distempered outbursts, were as unacceptable as tying one's garters in public.

If Moderation was Miss Meadow's rule for the future duchesses and marchionesses, Less was the motto for their teachers: less time, less money, less privacy, and much less spirit. The girls inside the office wore lace collars on their trim uniforms and colorful ribbons in their hair. Miss Swann wore unrelieved brown bombazine hanging on her five-foot-eight-inch too-thin frame, with her streaky blond hair scraped back into a tight, unbecoming bun. She sat with her hands folded meekly in her lap, her blue eyes downcast, a quiet, obedient, colorless female.

If the debutantes-in-training were invited to lavish afternoon teas, preparing them for society, the teachers were expected to spend that time with their books, preparing for the next day's lessons. The pupils had two hours of free time after dinner to practice their womanly arts, such as gossiping and discussing the newest fashion magazines. The instructors needed those hours to practice housekeeping, for no maid was assigned to see to their clothes or accommodations. This was also the only time of day for Miss Swann to practice her own music, to maintain her own skills.

The young ladies in the upper classes, those soon to make fashionable marriages, it was assumed—nay, devoutly prayed—were given rooms of their own. The lucky instructors shared rooms; the younger, less favored had curtained alcoves in the smaller girls' dormitories. This was why Miss Swann, at twenty-four the youngest teacher at the academy, carried her precious letter in her pocket, rather than let the eight twelve-year-olds whose room she shared also share her personal business.

And if, finally, those pampered darlings of the *ton*—this was *not* a charity school; there were no scholarship students here—received the plump Miss Meadow's chirps and cheery head-bobs, earning her the nickname Meadowlark, the teachers received cold, short shrift. That kindly, smiling appearance hid a fact which Miss Swann knew well: inside Miss Meadow's dumpling of a body beat a heart so coal-black it could stoke the fires of hell a good long while. Which was why she sat up even straighter, her back not touching the chair, and nervously tucked an errant lock back into its bun as two girls left Miss Meadow's office giggling and chatting. Only one of the girls gave Miss Swann the merest nod of recognition, and that likely because the music teacher's knock and request for an interview had occasioned another of Miss Meadow's favorite teaching methods, the Precept. To instill the proper attitude in her students, Miss Meadow constantly held up examples. Last year's graduate who had snapped up the heir to a dukedom in her very first season was held as the ideal model of proper behavior. Contrariwise, a bad example was the well-dowered debutante who, some years after her graduation, had cast aside all of Miss Meadow's teachings and her parents' orders, to marry an Ineligible man. A half-pay officer, he had left her as soon as her money was spent. The story was often embellished by titters and whispers after lights-out, to tales no proper young lady should know, but all did.

Tonight's Precept had been Miss Cristabel Swann, or what not to become. Miss Swann's mother had married a—deep breath—Second Son. Now their daughter, gently bred, properly educated, was fallen on hard times. Like most of the teachers at Miss Meadow's Select Academy, she was a lady without prospects, a spinster of twenty-four who had not and never would make a good marriage. Was this what the girls wanted for themselves or their daughters? Heaven forbid! The last girl out gave Miss Swann a look that mingled pity with the superior knowledge that *she* would never make the same mistake, as she told Miss Swann that she could go in now.

"Well, what is it?" growled little Miss Meadow from

behind her cherrywood desk. She did not ask Miss Swann to sit or offer her refreshment, although the tea tray was right in front of her.

Trying not to feel enormously tall and gawky, looking down at the headmistress, and trying particularly not to let her stomach rumble at the almond tarts in their silver dish, Miss Swann replied: "I have received a letter from my uncle's solicitor in London. He—"

Miss Meadow had her pudgy little hand out. Cristabel did not even think to refuse. She drew the letter from her pocket and handed it over, continuing despite the interruption, while the other woman smoothed out the rumpled, slightly soiled document. "He wishes to consult with me as soon as possible, he writes, concerning the estate of my Uncle Charles."

"Baron Harwood, eh?" Miss Meadow gabbled to herself. "There's no heir to the title, so the Crown will recall the entailed holdings." (She knew her Debrett's better than her Bible. No, Debrett's *was* her Bible. The gossip columns were her hymnal.) "He was a ne'er-do-well anyway, a gamester. There won't be anything left," she mumbled, holding the page right under her nose to see better, or to sniff out any advantage to herself in it. There wasn't any, so she lost interest and handed the letter back. "Too bad."

"Too bad" seemed a fairly cold remark to offer someone whose uncle has passed on to his final and just reward, but Cristabel herself was not precisely grief-stricken, so she merely accepted it as a comment on the late baron's luck, or lack of it. "Thank you," she said, adding, "the lawyer did speak of an estate, however."

"Nothing of value, you can be sure. No, if there were a vast fortune, the solicitor would certainly have come in person. If there were even a modest inheritance, he would have sent a carriage. At the very least, if there were anything at all, he would have enclosed coach fare. That's the way these men of business think. No, he just wants your permission to dispose of some gimcrack family stuff. You'll write back telling him to sell the lot and send you a check."

Cristabel twisted the letter in her long, thin hands. "Perhaps there is a portrait of my father I would like to have, or an heirloom I might wish to keep."

"Would you?" Miss Meadow considered. "Yes, I suppose you would." The fact that Miss Meadow harbored no such mawkish sentiments was evident in her tone. "In that case, you must request a list of the items for your perusal. Really, Miss Swann, you could have figured this out for yourself. My teachers cannot be so featherheaded as that. Now, I am quite busy." Her beady eyes flicked to the almond tarts. "Will that be all?"

Miss Swann licked her lips and took a deep breath. "I . . . I thought I might go to London."

Miss Meadow sighed. This was really getting quite tedious. "The summer break shall be upon us in a few months. I had thought you might be more useful here with the day students, but perhaps you could escort one of the girls home for her vacation and fit a few days in London into your return schedule. Though why anyone would want to visit the metropolis in the heat of July is beyond me. Still, it might be educational for you, something to pass on to your students. Yes, we might consider it." Miss Meadow selected a paper from her desk—on the other side from the tea things—and started to read. Her forehead puckered as if in concentration.

Miss Swann had accompanied one of her more favorite students to the girl's parents' estate some Christmases past, and she was not about to do so again. Invited to stay, Cristabel was housed with the servants; requested to play the pianoforte, she was hidden behind a screen of potted ferns to entertain the family's house guests. Nor was she anxious to remain at the school all summer, giving remedial music lessons to those young ladies whose families were in Bath for July or August, away from that same London heat. The girls resented lessons in the summer; Miss Swann resented that the other teachers were permitted to visit their own families during the long break, even though she had no one to visit. That was nothing to do with today's issue. Cristabel cleared her throat.

Miss Meadow stopped pretending to read. "Yes, Miss Swann, I *shall* consider your request." She looked down. Then up. "Was there something else?"

"I thought I might go to London now. That is, as soon as possible. Miss Macklin could take my place with the younger girls, and the older girls could practice their repertoires for the week or so I'd be gone."

The paper was slammed down on the desk, making the teapot and Miss Swann both jump. "Oh, you did, did you? Think you could just go jauntering off to town for a holiday? Of all the maggoty notions! I would expect such an idea from one of the younger pupils. Who did you think would take Miss Macklin's place teaching voice? The drawing teacher—or perhaps the scullery maid? Miss Swann, I expected better of you, certainly more loyalty to the academy. Your idea is a total impossibility. Total, I am sure. I have said you may go on this fruitless quest during the summer, despite the inconvenience it shall cause in the class scheduling. I think that is very generous on my part, do not you?"

"Yes, Miss Meadow." Cristabel did not say that the middle-aged proprietress could herself take part in the education of her pupils, or that the scullery maid could likely teach the young ladies something more important in life than the proper way to balance a teacup. She did not even comment on Miss Meadow's generosity, which had never extended to giving Cristabel a share in the exorbitant fees charged for those private summer music lessons. The only thing she did say, on her way out, was "Yes, Miss Meadow."

The headmistress made no answer as Cristabel closed the door behind her and fled. Not upstairs to "her" room, where those little imps-of-Satan would wheedle her upset and disappointment out of her. Instead she glided across the hall, slowly and gracefully even in her distress, to the music room where she would be undisturbed. Heavens knew, none of the girls ever practiced their music without being assigned.

It was here, with the pianoforte and the harp, that Miss Swann was used to escaping from the drudgery and petty nastiness. Here even the specter of Miss Meadow evaporated into the mist of music and daydreams. And Miss Swann *did* have dreams.

Her musings weren't like the debutante dreams her students were forever weaving, all fancy gowns, grand balls, handsome lords. Cristabel's were much more modest, like the vision she had of just one new dress. Muslin, she and Herr Bach picked out. Cornflower blue to match her eyes. Or maybe pink to give some color to her wan indoor complexion—anything but the brown, gray, black, or navy which were all she was permitted to wear. This was a possible dream, of course, one she might someday attain without touching her meager life savings. She could save the extra money by giving up her library subscription. The books she took out on her twice-monthly half days were mostly for the entertainment of her charges upstairs anyway, so they would lie abed quietly listening to her read, instead of raising a rumpus and Miss Meadow's wrath.

Cristabel had another dream, this one not nearly so easy to translate into reality, with or without any amount of cheeseparing. Here, lost in her music, she saw herself in a tiny cottage with a kitchen garden out back with flowers, sweet peas, perhaps, on a trellis in the front— and a nice, quiet, smiling gentleman to love and cherish her. Maybe a young barrister or haberdasher's assistant would spot her in her cornflower blue dress. He would fall in love and marry her, just for herself, despite her plain looks and lack of dowry. Maybe he would notice her at the lending library, unless, of course, she stopped using the library in order to save enough to buy the dress. If she went in her usual heavy, dark gowns, though, he would see only a washed-out, pinched-looking old maid. Ah well, so her dreams needed polishing. So did the new Mozart piece she was memorizing.

The problem, of course—with her dreams, not her music—was that Miss Swann hadn't always lived a life of endless monotony and servility, with a future as bleak as a Bath winter. Once she'd had a loving, happy home, with no luxuries, to be sure, but no lacks, either. Her father was the well-respected vicar in a small village where his little family had all they wanted and enjoyed what they had. Reverend Swann had died when Cristabel was sixteen, forcing his wife and daughter to eke out a meager living as best two gently bred females could, living in rented rooms and giving music lessons. Still, they had each other, but just for a year. At her mother's death, Cristabel considered herself fortunate to gain a position with Miss Meadow's school, teaching the youngest girls their do-re-mi's. Who knew what would have become of her else? Certainly her Uncle Charles hadn't answered her plea for help. She was not precisely ungrateful to Miss Meadow, these seven years later, but she couldn't help wishing that someday her life would change. She couldn't help fearing, though, that sometimes someday never came.

That was before the letter. Now, if the letter had just arrived, and she'd gone straightaway into Miss Meadow's office with it, then she would likely have done precisely as her employer advised. She would have written a polite reply to the solicitor. But she'd had the letter for two days. Last night one of her girls was sick, from too many candied cherries smuggled in somehow. And today was Patron Day at the school, when various of the Bath dowagers visited the establishment to have their sponsorship rewarded with an afternoon of musical renditions, poetry recitations, needlework and watercolor exhibits, and tea with Miss Meadow and some of the upper girls. The school benefited from the association with the *ton,* the girls learned more about the polite world, and the patronesses got to feel they were making an unselfish contribution to society, without having to touch their checkbooks or anything dirty. If they wished to feel particularly magnanimous, they could even invite one or two of the senior girls to their homes for an afternoon call, especially if they had an impecunious nephew on the lookout for a rich wife. Anyway, Miss Meadow had been much too busy with the grand visitors to bother about the concerns of her most junior instructress. So Miss Swann had had the extra time to commit the letter to memory and to dream.

Think of castles in the sky; Cristabel built a full-blown fantasy palace! The town house in Grosvenor Square, a sedate older lady to act as chaperone and make introductions to the ladies of the *ton* who might remember her mother. Pretty dresses—a whole closet full—and a cheerful little maid to take care of them. Music—all she wanted, operas, concerts, musicales at . . . at Carlton House with the Prince! Why not, for Miss Cristabel Swann, heiress of Harwood House? Even if Uncle Charles had only left her a jointure, and she had to give music lessons to supplement her income . . . Even if Uncle Charlie had just *remembered* her, if someone cared.

She couldn't simply write a letter. She couldn't let the dream die, not when it might be her only chance, ever.

Miss Swann straightened her already firm spine. She raised her pointed chin and this time marched back across the hallway to Miss Meadow's office.

"What now, Miss Swann?"

"Miss Meadow, I *wish* to go to London."

"What is that to the purpose? I wish to waltz with the king!"

Cristabel almost lost track of her thoughts, picturing this tiny harridan dancing with the mad king, in his nightshirt, if rumors were true. She shook her head. "Miss Meadow, I wish to go now."

"And I wish this conversation at an end. One more word and you shan't go to London at all, not now, not this summer. Not ever. Is that clear?"

"Yes, Miss Meadow, but—"

"I am finding your behavior impertinent and unbecoming in the extreme. I shall have to reconsider renewing your contract for next year."

"Yes, Miss Meadow, but this year or rather next week . . ."

"If you say 'but' to me one more time, young lady, one

more word about this matter, I shall consider terminating your employment altogether."

There it was then, Cristabel's choice, and she didn't even hesitate. If Cristabel had paused, had thought about the gamble she was taking, she knew she wouldn't do it, couldn't do it. She did it.

"I am going to London, to see my uncle's man of business as soon as arrangements can be made."

While Miss Swann stood calmly, her hands clasped neatly in front of her, the headmistress grew proportionately more disturbed. Miss Meadow pursed her lips and narrowed her eyes, making her resemble a petulant peahen more than ever. She flapped her pudgy hands in the air before holding them up and enumerating her points on the fleshy fingers. "Number one," she squawked, "if you leave, do not expect to return. Two, do not expect a reference. Three, do not expect this quarter's wages, since you have not finished the term. And four, do not expect that I shall regret your departure."

"I thought you were satisfied with my work. I am sorry."

"Sorry? We'll see who's sorry! Or did you think I couldn't find someone else to replace you as music instructor? There's many a gentlewoman who could fill your position admirably, young lady, and thank me for the chance."

That this was patently untrue—that there were many, or any other wellborn ladies who would perform Miss Swann's duties so well, so cheaply, and so uncomplainingly—did not bother the angry old besom, as long as Miss Swann believed. it. Cristabel did believe that the pupils would hardly notice if an orangutan were instructing them at the pianoforte. The younger girls pounded out their endless scales, unmercifully. The older ones got through their requisite Handel pieces so they might appear accomplished at house parties. Perhaps an ape would have better luck teaching them to appreciate the music, or even read the score, when they could barely get through *La Belle Assemblee* without referring to the pictures.

A replacement harpist might be a rarer commodity, and Miss Meadow did like the image of her pupils, dressed all in white, performing for Patron Days. Still, Cristabel was sure the threat was true: she would be replaced before she reached London, and some other poor unfortunate would be helping those spoiled darlings look like angels—on her harp! The instrument had been Cristabel's mother's and had been one reason for her finding employment at such an early age. It had also been used and abused, scuffed, and strummed to shrieking by seven years of careless girls, for free.

Cristabel smiled. She actually grinned, erasing the frown lines and momentarily changing the drawn, tired woman into a charming girl. The impertinence of it made Miss Meadow so furious she gobbled down an apricot tart. Cristabel's words made her choke on it: "I shall remove as soon as I can pack my belongings and arrange transport to London for myself . . . and the harp."

"The harp?" Crumbs spewed all over. The beaky mouth twisted into a grimace. "Miss Swann, sometimes I forget the impetuosity of youth. I shall permit you twenty-four hours to reconsider this rash decision. I shall also expect an apology on my desk tomorrow evening, then we may consider the matter finished. I suggest you retire now and deliberate on your future."

Cristabel curtsied. She closed the door behind her and leaned against it. Twenty-four hours. One day.

"Godfrey," she called out to the half-deaf night porter stationed by the front door, "I need a hackney carriage to take me to the nearest posting house. Tell the driver to be here in an hour." Just in case Godfrey hadn't heard, or any of those touseled heads now leaning over the upstairs railing, or Miss Meadow herself, cramming tea cakes down her throat, Cristabel repeated, only louder and slower: "I need a carriage. Going to London. In one hour."

"Are you really leaving, Miss Swann?" one of the dormitory girls wanted to know.

"Yes, I am traveling to London within the hour, so you must not pester me with your questions. I have to pack."

"Janine said the maid said that she heard your uncle died and left you a fortune. Is that true?"

"Janine should not gossip with the maids or listen to keyhole rumors."

"But is it true?" another girl asked. All eight of them were clustered around Cristabel.

"It's something like that. No, it's nothing like that, just family matters. Now let me pass. Everyone back in bed, quickly, before Miss Meadow comes to see what the commotion is."

"You mean to supervise your packing like she did with that maid who left last month," giggled little Lady Jessica, scrambling for her bed in a flurry of bare feet and billowy white nightgown. "To make sure you don't leave with any of the school's forks or spoons."

"Maybe she'll check to see you're not stuffing one of *us* into your trunk to hold for ransom."

"Whatever would I want with one of you?" Cristabel teased as she walked past the eight beds in a row, neatening a cover or tucking a curl into a lacy nightcap. "I thought I was going to London to get away from you plaguey children. Besides, you have been reading far too many Minerva Press novels, all of you. I'm sure Miss Meadow will blame me for that, too."

They all laughed. Indeed, it was Cristabel who brought the gothic romances back from the lending library for the girls, tucked between volumes of sermons and improving works. She felt the girls were better off reading something, anything at all, rather than nothing. "Hush now," she said, kissing the last girl on the forehead. "I must get ready."

"She will, you know," a small, serious voice called from across the room. "She'll blame everything on you. She'll blacken your character and use you as a bad example."

"She'll say she had to dismiss you because your conduct was unbecoming to the school's image."

"She'll say . . . she'll say you aren't a lady."

There was a moment's silence as they all, Cristabel included, contemplated this death knell of Miss Swann's reputation. Then came a firm assertion: "Well, I won't believe it," followed by a whole chorus of, "me neither's." Then Miss Swann quietly answered, "Thank you, girls. I won't believe it either."

There was very little to pack. The nights were still cold so she would wear her warmest dress, the gray merino, and her shawl so the spots wouldn't show, her wool cloak and boots, and the only bonnet she owned. Her other dresses, slippers, nightclothes, and underthings all fit in the portmanteau she used as a laundry basket, with room to spare for a few of her favorite books saved from her father's library. She'd like to give the rest to the other teachers, especially Miss Macklin, the voice instructor, who was closest to Cristabel in age. She knew the staff would be cowering in their rooms, however, lest Miss

Meadow's disfavor rub off on them. No, singling out Miss Macklin would not be a kindness.

That left only her comb and brush, inlaid in ivory with her mother's initials, and the miniature portraits of her parents. As she carefully wrapped the double silver frame in her spare nightgown, she couldn't help worrying if her parents would have approved. Would her proper mama have deplored her lack of mourning for the dead or noticed, in fact, that Cristabel was nearly ecstatic at her uncle's demise, already considering how to spend his money? No, Mrs. Swann was no hypocrite and had never approved of her brother-in-law or his way of life, especially after the vicar's death, when Lord Harwood did not even extend the common courtesy of a condolence letter to the widow, much less an offer of assistance to her and her daughter. But would they think she was being a fool to leave the security of her position at the school or, worse, becoming a gambler like Uncle Charles? Gentle Papa had always said it was in the Harwood blood, and they mustn't blame Uncle Charles for his failings but should pray for him instead.

Cristabel closed the fastenings on the suitcase. Her decision felt so right, but she couldn't help whispering, "Papa, pray for me."

Chapter Three

The decision still felt right. Miss Swann felt awful. Odysseus may have had a worse journey, but she doubted it. To start with, she found at the posting inn that she could ride on the mail coach, but her harp could not. That is, it could be wrapped in oilskin and tied to the back or tossed on the top of the carriage to face the rain, fog, and cold of foul, early spring weather, the road dirt, and the ill-handling of reluctant postboys. Instead, she was compelled to hire a post chaise and driver, and postillions at the stages. The cost of this was so high that Cristabel was forced to economize in her food, lodgings, and tips, which only earned her worse food, lodgings, and treatment. Innkeepers and their employees did not look kindly on single women traveling alone, especially long Megs who were too thin, wore faded, funereal clothes, and had a heavy instrument that needed carting in and out of carriages to boot, lest it be affected by the dampness of the night despite its covering. Miss Swann was too proper to make sport of and too poor to respect, so she was given neglect and insolence. There were tiny rooms with clammy, unaired sheets and no fires, barely warm meals of whatever was left over, broken-down, mismatched horses so the ride was longer yet and bumpy—and sullen unfriendliness. She even found herself missing the girls at Miss Meadow's school!

The first night Cristabel was still buoyed by the sheer glory of her great adventure. She, Cristabel Swann, had had the courage to defy Miss Meadow and was actually on her way to a better future. She didn't even mind having to sleep as best she could in a hard chair in the inn's common room, all of the bedrooms being taken. She was too excited to sleep anyway and, too, it was cheaper. There was a great deal to see, with carriages and travelers coming and going, so it wasn't until much later that she remembered the knotted handkerchief one of the girls in her room had pressed into her hand as she was leaving. Inside, Cristabel found three half-melted bonbons, two copper pennies, a pink silk rose with frayed petals, a stub of a pencil, and a much-folded watercolor of the academy, possibly. Warmed by the children's thoughtfulness despite the dying fire in the drafty room, Cristabel poked the rose through the limp brim of her ugly black straw bonnet and used the pencil to calculate her finances on the back of the painting.

On the second night, the bonbons tasted like manna, and Miss Swann wished there were three more at least, or just one of Miss Meadow's almond tarts. The results on the back of the painting were as depressing as those on the front, and Cristabel was beginning to feel headachy and stuffy-nosed. It was also the first night in nearly eight years that she had had a room all to herself, except for the wildlife she was sure inhabited the inn's beds. She was independent and free—and all alone in the world.

After that things got worse: the weather, and so the roads, her cold—thank heavens for the gift handkerchief—and her finances.

By the time Miss Swann finally reached London, so

many days later she lost count, she was as damp and
bedraggled as the rose drooping onto her forehead. Her
nose was all red and her eyes were streaming. Her throat
was so scratchy it hurt just to breathe the London air. Besides, one wasn't supposed to be able to see the air, was
one? She was in no condition to face the solicitor that afternoon, if he hadn't already left his offices, and she
doubted she had enough money left for a respectable
London hotel, if she could find one that would accept her.
She knew better than to put up at a coaching house, for
what was barely respectable for a single lady on the road
was actually dangerous for an unprotected woman in the
city, so she did the only thing possible. She asked the
driver to take her to Harwood House, Grosvenor Square.

She recognized a few landmarks from her guidebooks,
but recalled nothing from the two childhood visits she
had made with her parents many years ago, until they
reached the house itself. Set back from the road across
from the park, it was neither as large nor as well kept as
its neighbors. Of brown stone, it was a fairly unprepos-
sessing, drab building, with only one thing to recommend
it—it was home!

Cristabel staggered down from the carriage and
dragged her portmanteau out with her while the driver
struggled with the harp, grunting and cursing the whole
way up the front walk and the seven marble steps. The
new heiress lifted the heavy knocker, then looked up at
the Harwood arms over the door, all swans, trees, and
swords, while she waited. And waited.

A young footman finally answered the door, hastily
pulling the napkin from his livery's collar and wiping his
mouth, which then hung open at the sight of a draggle-

tailed female standing on his master's doorstep. 'Cor, 'n it being the butler's day off asides.

"I am Miss Swann," Cristabel announced, and received no more recognition—or less bemusement—than if she'd just identified herself as St. George. "Lord Harwood's niece?" Cristabel's inflection meant, "There, now will you give me proper welcome?" The young servant, though, took her question to mean she didn't rightly know who she was. Dotty female, come knocking on strangers' doors. Whisht, what's to do? The coachman was no help, a-bumping through the entryway past both Cristabel and the footman.

"Where do you want this here thing, then, lady? I ain't paid for standin' here jawing."

Cristabel looked to the befuddled footman, got no response. Really, this was too much. She could understand a caretaker staff not being up to the standards of a gentleman's residence, but leaving simple-minded hirelings in charge of an empty house was unconscionable. What if she'd been a thief? She'd have to have a talk with her uncle's solicitor very shortly. Meanwhile she, and the footman, had followed the burdened coachman across the black-and-white marble squares into the wide hall. There were many doors leading off the hallway on either side of a central stairway, all shut, and Cristabel could not remember the order of the rooms, much less know their conditions.

"Put it down by the stairs for now," she directed, "and I'll decide later which room is most suitable." She placed her portmanteau near the harp with a frown for the footman, who had neglected to relieve her of the baggage. Poor want-wit, he was scratching his head as if he'd never seen a harp before.

Poor Floyd, for that was the footman's name, had in-

deed never seen the like, some old crow looking like
she'd been dragged backward through a briar hedge, a-
moving into 'is lordship's vestibule like she owned the
place. Butler'd have his head, he would. And as for 'is
lordship . . . Well, Floyd figured as how he'd better get
some help. But how could he leave this attics-to-let female alone? He edged toward the stairs, which was a sure
sign of his distress, that he'd so much as think of using
the front stairway, instead of the rear. He had to reach his
master's man Sparling upstairs while the corkbrained
woman was busy paying off the driver.

There went almost the last of Cristabel's money, and
good riddance to the coachman, even more surly seeing
the size of his tip. But heavens, the feebleminded manser-
vant was sidling across the hall, eyeing her slantwise.
Cristabel didn't think she wanted to spend the night in the
house alone with just this simple fellow.

"You there," she called, speaking very slowly and
carefully, "do you think you could find your way to the
solicitor's office? It's on Fleet Street. F-l-e-e-t Street. Do
you think you can remember?"

Floyd nodded, desperately.

"Good, good. You're to ask for Mr. Worbigger and ask
him to attend Miss Swann here as soon as possible, all
right?"

Floyd decided to humor the madwoman, nip out the
front, scoot around to the kitchen door, and up the back
way to find Sparling. "Yes'm," he said, trying to scuttle
toward the entryway without turning his back on her.

"You're sure now, you understand the message?"

"Mr. Worbigger, Fleet Street. Miss Swann, here."

"Fine. I'll wait in there," Cristabel said, turning to
what she assumed was the front parlor, the first door on
the right.

Floyd gasped. "In there?"

"Don't worry, I shan't consider the room's condition," she said, her hand on the doorknob.

"But, but his lordship's in—"

"In here?" Cristabel dropped the handle like a hot coal. Her dead uncle was still laid out at home! She shuddered. "You mean they were waiting for me?"

Floyd took another look at the frumpy clothes, the stringy hair, the red nose and eyes. "I doubt it, ma'am."

"Then why in heaven's name haven't they buried him yet?"

"Because he ain't dead yet, though it were a near thing."

Not dead! Her Uncle Charles was still alive, and he'd had Mr. Worbigger send for her! "I better go right in to him then."

Floyd swallowed hard, his Adam's apple bobbing above the uniform's collar. "Oh ma'am, I wouldn't do that. Oh no. His lordship'd have my head. That is, he, um, mightn't be fit for company. Right, he ain't ready to receive you now. Perhaps his valet will know . . . er, will see if the master . . . Why don't I just go fetch him, miss?"

Cristabel sank down on a chair outside the room, dazed. She just couldn't believe it. After all those years, Uncle Charlie had remembered her. Old and ailing, near to death, he wanted family near him. Well, Cristabel would shower him with her care. She would read him the newspapers, fetch his medicines, brighten his remaining days with music and flowers and—

And there were noises coming from behind the closed door, moans they were, she was sure. He needed her!

"I'm coming, Uncle," she cried, tearing open the door and racing into the room.

There he was, fallen on the floor by the sofa, too near the fireplace. His head was all bandaged, and he was struggling with the blanket entangling him.

"Here I am, Uncle Ch—Ch—Oh, my Lord!" For there were two people under the blanket. The one not wearing bandages, and a paisley robe, was a stunning redhead not wearing much except rouge. She looked up at Cristabel, smiled and waved. Miss Swann should have fled; she knew that. She should have fainted at least. No such luck. Her feet were stuck to the carpet with the glue of impending hysteria. All she could do was shut her eyes. "Uncle," she whispered, swaying.

"What in bloody hell!"

"Uncle!" Cristabel's eyes popped wide at the language, screwed shut again at the sight of the gentleman groping for the sash of his robe.

"I am nobody's blasted uncle!"

Wrapped in the blanket, the redhead helped him, then gathered a pile of clothing and what remained of the dignity of the situation. She left with a cheery " 'Ta," which both of the others ignored.

The man couldn't possibly be Uncle Charles, Cristabel saw now. The broad shoulders, erect bearing, all bespoke a much younger man, and the dark curls showing at the vee of his robe, well, it wasn't Uncle Charles, that was for sure.

"If you are not my uncle, then what are you doing here?"

"Ma'am, unless you are as blindfolded as I, it must be obvious what I am—or was—doing here!" he thundered. "But what in God's name are you doing here?"

Cristabel blushed—thank heavens the insufferable brute couldn't see that—and drew herself up to her considerable height, which was still inches shorter than this blackguard. "I am Miss Cristabel Swann," she announced, "and I demand to know what you are doing in my house."

"Your house? Your house?" Captain Chase rubbed at his forehead. Damn these bandages anyway, he couldn't even tell if the deranged female had a weapon. What a blasted situation; he'd have that fool footman's liver and lights and—"Did you say Miss Swann?"

"Miss Cristabel Swann, Lord Charles Harwood's niece."

The baron's preachy old maid? Oh, Lord, was that who saw him and what's-her-name? What a coil.

"Miss Swann, I am afraid there is a misunderstanding here. Your late uncle— You do know Lord Harwood is deceased, don't you?"

"I had assumed as much before—"

He held up a hand. "Please, let me continue. Before his death Lord Harwood took part in a card game, a lot of card games, and he wagered this house, among other things. He lost, and I now own Harwood House."

"No, that's a lie, he couldn't have." This, this libertine could not be telling the truth.

The muscles in the man's jaw clenched, visible even under the dark, concealing stubble there. "Ma'am, are you accusing me of being a liar?"

Cristabel fumbled in her reticule with numb fingers. "I have a letter here from his solicitor about the estate. See, Mr. Worbigger writes that—"

"Miss Swann," he ground out, "I cannot *see* anything. Your uncle lost this house to me in a gentlemen's card game, and that is that!"

Cristabel was extremely tired of being shouted at by this large person whose behavior to this point had not given her any reason for considering him a gentleman.

Besides, she had no knowledge of how to navigate the tricky shoals of male honor. In fact, she knew very little of men at all and knew only Miss Meadow's lectures on the evils of the city. "That's impossible," she shouted back, unwisely as it turned out. "The game must have been crooked."

"Now I'm a cheat as well as a liar? No man would dare—"

"And a libertine and a housebreaker to boot! And I dare!"

"If you weren't hiding behind your petticoats, you blasted woman, I'd . . . I'd . . ." He didn't know what he'd do, but it wouldn't be pretty. His hands were itching to wrap around something and shake it or squeeze it or—

"And a bully, too!" Cristabel raged. "This whole thing is a hum, and I demand you leave instantly before I call the watch. I may be a green country girl, and Uncle may have been a . . . a loose screw, but even I know there's no way he could have lost an honest card game to you."

"What, are you calling me a moonling now? I wonder what's next on your charming list? Perhaps murderer. If ever I was tempted, Miss Swann, this is it! Once and for all, your uncle lost fairly."

"Forgive me for being blunt, Mr. Whoever-you-are, but I refuse to believe that a man who cannot see his cards is a match for anyone but another blind man!"

That brought him up short. She was right, of course, and his incivility was inexcusable despite the provocation.

"My apologies, miss. I am Captain Chase, and I was not so, ah, incapacitated at the time. I realize this has been difficult for you and, with your permission, I shall send for Lord Harwood's solicitor and my own man of business to settle this. Will you excuse me, ma'am?"

With her murmured concurrence, he bolted, recalled to the fact that he was in his undress. Gads, he could feel her disapproval like a cold draft. No woman had made him feel so foolish or so out-of-countenance small since one of his cousin's governesses had reprimanded him for some boyhood prank.

"Sparling," he bellowed. "Fall out. I need you for some errands, on the double." The captain strode across the hall toward the stairwell—and tripped over the harp.

"What in blazes now?" he yelled, throwing off Miss Swann's arm. He groped at the instrument's shape, then scrambled back to his feet with one hand. (The other clutched his robe together.) "What kind of addle-pated fool leaves a damned harp in the middle of the floor?" A string of curses filled the air then, describing the improbable parentage of the person responsible.

Luckily, Miss Swann did not understand the half of them, only enough to know this ill-bred savage was storming at *her*. She was also exhausted and sick, and sick at heart, or she would be if she let herself think about it, so she answered more or less in kind: "I left it there, you . . . you profligate, because there was no one in this ill-run house to direct me. And it wouldn't have been in your way if you had waited for help instead of going off all half-cocked. Furthermore, I'll thank you not to use such language in my presence, although I suppose it's only to be expected from such an unmannered wastrel and womanizer."

"Half-cocked, is it?" Chase ranted, furious at his clumsiness, the blasted bandages, and most of all the dratted female who was witness to this debacle, if not the cause of it. "Ma'am," he said, knowing he was wrong again, "a dried-up old prune like you wouldn't know—"

Cristabel gasped. "I never—"

And Captain Chase shouted, "Well maybe you should!"

A great many similar pleasantries were exchanged, hers in a raspy, straining screech, his in a booming quarterdeck baritone. Luckily they were shouting too loudly to hear the other's remarks, beyond rakehell, muckworm, and basket-scrambler on her part, and shrew, shark-bait, and self-righteous marplot on his.

When they ran out of breath, the captain headed toward the stairs again, this time carefully feeling his way by lightly touching the familiar objects along the walls. Tables, chairs, the harp. Aha! He stepped around the instrument, tossing Miss Swann a triumphant smirk. And tripped over her portmanteau.

Chapter Four

A man desperate enough over his debts to kill himself is not likely to leave his kin in much better straits. So Cristabel reasoned after hearing the dismal news from the housekeeper, sometime later. She'd been sitting huddled and forlorn, forgotten by everyone, it seemed, though she could hear that madman's shouted orders and stompings. Doors slammed and servants scurried by, but if it wasn't her house, Cristabel would starve before she'd presume to ask one of the servants for something to eat, if that man hadn't offered. She would just sit, waiting for Mr. Worbigger to arrive to tell her that there was something, anything, for her in her uncle's will.

"He didn't even leave a will," the housekeeper, Mrs. Witt, told Cristabel, "didn't make one provision for the staff. Lord knows he hadn't paid them in months anyway, so they oughtn't to have been surprised. Still, it were up to the captain to make good, which he did, pensioning the lot off with the game's winnings and starting fresh, so to speak, so you mustn't judge him by today, you know."

They were sitting in the kitchen, Cristabel sipping some blessedly hot tea with honey to soothe her throat, and eating scones. Mrs. Witt had been horrified to find a damp, distressed lady sitting in the hallway, for who knows how long, and had whisked her off to her own tiny sitting room, "for I don't think the master'd be any pleased to meet you in the upper halls right now, from the sound of things, begging your pardon."

Cristabel grimaced. "If I had my way, I would never meet with that bounder again. A more discourteous, shameless . . . why, I don't know how you can tolerate such immorality. This very afternoon—"

"Well, it's not what a body could want in a proper household, but he did give most of the staff the afternoon off, you know. It's not as if he treats this as bachelor's quarters, in the way of things, not fouling his own nest, so to speak. But a gentleman must have his pleasures, you know. Why, Mr. Witt what were—"

Cristabel put the cup down, hard.

"No, I don't suppose you do. But the master can't get out and about, naturally, and him being so resty right now, having that nasty surgery and so long recuperating, it's no wonder he's a mite rackety. We're all hoping he'll settle down a bit, now that he's got so many new responsibilities."

Cristabel was doubtful. Tigers didn't change their spots, did they? Or was it leopards? It didn't matter. The blackguard had stolen *her* inheritance, honestly if not honorably, and it was doubtful Mr. Worbigger was coming to refute the dastard's claim. No, she only had to wait for the pittance the lawyer would likely bring, then she would never have to see the arrogant, immoral cad again.

"Nothing? There is nothing?"

The lawyers had arrived, Mr. Worbigger with a secretary and a sheaf of papers, and a Mr. Gould, of Gould, Gould, Woods, and Gould. They were seated in her uncle's library, where the men were immediately offered refreshment. The contrast to her own treatment only added to Cristabel's hostility and humiliation. The captain was dressed presentably, although his clothes were as loose as his morals, Cristabel noted disdainfully, and he was still scruffy and unshaven beneath the bandages. Mrs. Witt had mentioned an operation, however, so she charitably reconsidered and acknowledged that her criticism was partly based on resentment. The swine was able to look respectable despite his activities, while she had been unable to do much to improve her own appearance. She had tried to neaten up, with Mrs. Witt's help, but there wasn't a lot to be done. She couldn't very well wash her hair, and her other dresses were just as rumpled, from being packed, and just as dowdy. There was nothing for it, except to be thankful that one of the men, at least, couldn't see her sorry state.

Mr. Worbigger "ahem-ed" for her attention, though how it could wander at a time like this was beyond her. Maybe she was delirious with the fever and this was all a bad dream. It must be, with the solicitor's droning voice explaining debentures and rights of entailment.

"You must see that the, ah, final dispersal of his lordship's estate was determined almost before the fatal card game. There were so many creditors that the sale of Harwood House itself would not have satisfied them. Lord Harwood must have decided that gambling with his only remaining asset was preferable to fleeing the country. Deplorable situation, but there it is."

"But if there were so many debts, how does it happen that Harwood House was not sold to pay them?"

It was Mr. Gould's turn to be patronizing: "My dear young lady, debts of honor must naturally precede those to merchants and bankers."

He didn't hear Cristabel's raspy mutter: "Naturally," but Captain Chase did. "Many of the debts were to moneylenders. Your uncle had been punting on tick for quite some time. I would have returned the property to him had he lived, but I saw no reason to benefit the usurers. Furthermore, it suited me to have a London residence." Chase was thinking of how glad he'd been to escape Perry's fussing during his long convalescence and the feeling of being a burden to his friend in the cramped quarters at the Albany. Cristabel was thinking of his using Harwood House for his raking. It was a good thing he couldn't see her face.

"But if . . . if my uncle had not made me a bequest, why did you send for me? You did not just inform me of his death, you know. You specifically mentioned an estate." Oh dear, her words made her seem like a vulture come to prey on the dead. She hadn't felt so mercenary, back in Bath. She hadn't been so poor, back in Bath.

"Ah yes, the little misunderstanding." Cristabel and the captain were in agreement for the first time that day. They both would cheerfully have boiled Mr. Worbigger in oil.

" 'Little misunderstanding,' like hell," mumbled Chase, none too softly. It had been enough to bring a ranting harridan to his doorstep.

" 'Little misunderstanding,' " Cristabel snorted, encouraging her to bank her future on an empty account.

Mr. Worbigger loosened his collar. "Yes, well, ahem, I did need to contact you concerning the entailment."

Cristabel sat straighter.

"No, no. It would not have benefited you in any case, the Harwood barony not having a distaff clause. That is, neither title nor properties could have passed through the female line. Lord Harwood broke the entailment at the occasion of your father's death, in any event. With no further possibility of a male heir, the Crown granted his pe-

tition." The solicitor cleared his throat. "I believe the
baron was a gaming partner of the king's. Notwithstand-
ing the entailment, I wished to apprise you that the title
could be reinstated for your son, or at such time you had
a son, pursuant to a request to the proper offices, which I
would be happy to undertake on your behalf."

"And the country estates? Harwood Hall?"

"Gone. Years ago, I'm afraid."

"Dashed basket-scrambler." For the second time that
day Cristabel agreed with her host. Her host, for pity's
sake.

"That's it, then?" Cristabel asked weakly, her voice almost gone with her hopes. "You requested my presence
in London to discuss an unclaimed title and an unborn
heir?"

"Ah, not entirely. There were those other debts, you
see. I had no current knowledge of your situation and felt
duty-bound to ascertain your circumstances."

"Why thank you. I appreciate your concern, though I
could have wished you'd written—"

"Yes, there was the possibility that you had married
well and your husband would be desirous of settling the
debts. Family honor and all that. I see that I was mistaken."

"What?" Cristabel gasped; the captain chuckled. He
was finally beginning to enjoy this, hearing the greedy,
managing female get her comeuppance.

"You are fortunate," he told her now, destroying whatever easing of hostilities there had been. "In less enlight-
ened times the heirs could be imprisoned for the family's
debts. Your school in Bath must be preferable to the
Fleet."

Mr. Gould tut-tutted. "Now, now, your lordship. You
mustn't let Miss Swann think an unfortunate niece could

be held to account for her uncle's debts. Not legally, at any rate."

"Quite the contrary," Cristabel rasped, glowering at her unseeing tormentor. "I'm sure the captain would enjoy having a helpless female imprisoned despite her innocence."

The joke wasn't quite so amusing. Chase held up his hand. "Enough, Miss Swann. I am tired of trading insults with you. You must be satisfied with the legitimacy of my claim to the house by now, and it seems Lord Harwood's man has no further business with you. With your permission, I'll have my carriage brought around, to convey you to a hotel. Gentlemen?"

It was too much for one to bear, it truly was. Not only hadn't her dreams come true, but her worst nightmares had! Cristabel was destitute, homeless, jobless, and friendless—and had to admit as much before this despicable scapegrace. She sniffled, whether from the head cold or the devastation she faced, she didn't know. "Thank you, Captain Chase, but I . . . I cannot afford the night's lodging."

Without even seeing the handwringing, he was embarrassed for her. He gruffly told her, "No matter. I can advance you the cost, and your fare back to Bath."

"I couldn't—"

"Don't be foolish, Miss Swann, I did more for your uncle's servants."

"You don't understand. I cannot go back to Bath. I lost my position by coming to London without permission."

"Of all the cockle-headed females! And you found fault with *my* behavior?" Chase exclaimed, loudly enough to cause Cristabel to wince. He was truly astounded that such a proper spinster could act so imprudently. If this was an example of the educators, it was no wonder young women were such featherbrains! "If you will not return to Bath, is there a friend to whom I might escort you?" He did not quite say "ship you off to."

"No sir, there is no one, I'm afraid."

"Then just what in bloody tarnation do you intend to do now?"

It was a good question, loud but good. Cristabel only wanted to leave London, with all of its dirt and smells and rakish, distempered gentlemen.

"I . . . I shall sell my harp," she announced into the silence after the captain's furious demand, "and travel to . . . to Brighton, perhaps," she improvised, "and seek a new position. Except I have no references."

The new silence had the sound of dismay, horror, disbelief, depending on the gentleman hearing her last words. Brighton, where the Regent and his cronies summered? A single woman, out in the world on her own, with no references, no money, no position? Unthinkable! Impossible! Absurd!

"Damn!" The last thing in the world Captain Chase wanted was another ball of shot in his head. The second-to-last thing he wanted was another dependent. Heaven knew it wasn't the money; he could pension off any number of indigent relations or old servants. But Miss Swann was neither relation nor servant—and she wasn't, by Jupiter, going to be his responsibility! The hundred and twenty men who had gone down with the *Invicta* had been his responsibility, and fighting the Admiralty, Parliament, and the War Office for help for their widows and orphans, *that* was his responsibility. All the tenants and their families at Stokely, those were his to worry about, not some acid-tongued, moralistic old maid with no more sense than a seasick cabin boy. So what in the world was he to do with Miss Swann and her blasted harp? He'd as soon consign the instrument to a watery grave, but Harwood's niece? Kenley's sweet, gentle mother didn't deserve such a fate as having this priggish female foisted on her as companion, nor could Chase think of anyone he disliked enough to inflict such a dreary burden on. But deuce, she was a lady, and every bone in his body, and his sorely aching head, reminded him that a gentleman could not turn his back on a damsel in distress, no matter the provocation.

"Mr. Gould? Mr. Worbigger?" It was a plea for help, man to man. The solicitors, gentlemen both, were thinking similar thoughts: What was going to happen to this frail, innocent child with her pretty, blue eyes and tired, valiant smile? She'd be swallowed alive in London, and finding her references for a position—forged if need be—would only commit her to a life of drudgery. They had no solutions.

Miss Swann herself was almost too numb to think, except that she had no wish to be beholden to Captain Chase. "Children in London must need music lessons. If you could direct me to an employment office . . ."

"Without references? Pigs would fly sooner." Perhaps Perry knew someone with a parcel of brats whose already nasty little minds couldn't be soured by such a prude.

Worbigger's spotty-faced young secretary had properly contributed nothing to the discussion beyond a deal of paper ruffling whenever his employer had mentioned clauses or creditors. No one else had any suggestions, though, so he tapped the solicitor on the shoulder.

"What is it, boy? No, don't whisper. If you know of a position or something, speak up."

Embarrassed, the youth stuttered: "C-couldn't she stay here? This p-place is so large." He waved his hand around to express endless rooms and space, and all the pages fell on the floor.

There were four vehement "No's." The lawyers deemed the idea so vastly improper that Mr. Gould frowned at Mr. Worbigger, who none so gently kicked his aide in the ankle, under cover of helping to retrieve the documents. A young gentlewoman sharing rooms with a confirmed bachelor? Never! Miss Swann was horrified at the thought; she wouldn't get a night's sleep, wondering if she were safe in her bed, in the same house with such a satyr. His lordship was visualizing the end of his days of peace and pleasure—before they'd nearly started. No, it would have to be his mother's, after all.

"What now, boy?" The assistant was too mortified to speak. Red-faced, he held out a paper. Mr. Worbigger read it, said "Hum," and handed it over to Mr. Gould. Mr. Gould settled his spectacles, read, and said "Hum."

"Hum? What is 'hum'? Have you found something?"

"Do you recall a bit of property in Kensington, my lord, er, Captain? I brought it to your attention when you were ill."

"Something, vaguely, You said there was a question but I needn't trouble over it for some time."

"Yes, that's it. It seems that when Lord Harwood wrote his voucher at Hazlip's he signed over the deeds to his London properties. Mr. Worbigger and I assumed he meant this property, Harwood House, and its contents. That was the nature of the wager, wasn't it?"

"Yes, yes. Go on."

"Well, some time after, during your early recuperation and before you had removed here, Mr. Worbigger and his—hurph—assistant came to collect his lordship's papers. Among them they discovered another deed, to a small house in Kensington."

"Why in the world would my uncle have another house in London?" Miss Swann wanted to know, to the lawyer's chagrin and Captain Chase's amusement.

"Do you know what a *bijou* is, ma'am?"

"A jewel? I don't see—"

"If your sensibilities can take much more enlightening in one day, suffice it to say your uncle had more respect for his house than I did and other vices beyond gambling." He couldn't see the blush, but he heard the quick intake of breath. Satisfied, he turned back to his man of business.

"Go on, Mr. Gould. Did you settle the ownership of the, ah, small house?"

"There's no question at all, sir. The house is yours. The uncertainty was if there were liens against it, and there were none that we could find. One of my clerks visited the property and found it had been turned into a boardinghouse. That was when I approached you, but you were not in condition to decide whether to keep the property, since it was in a decent enough location, or sell it, because it does not earn much in rental income."

Captain Chase was delighted. "Do you mean that I own an establishment in a respectable neighborhood, one that could even be self-supporting?"

"Indeed, sir, you do."

"Miss Swann, do you care to be a landlady? I'm confident you could make a go of it! You'd have a proper place to live and an income. I'm obviously in no state to oversee such an enterprise, so it appears the solution to both of our dilemmas!" Lord, what else could he say to convince her?

With the lawyers adding their encouragement, Miss Swann found herself and her harp on the other side of the door to Harwood House before the cat could lick its whiskers. Her head swimming, she clutched a pile of pound notes from the captain to help her get settled. Kenley Chase did not even listen to her vows to repay the money as soon as possible, considering a hundred pounds cheap at any reckoning to get that blasted woman out of his sight. Make that out of his life.

Chapter Five

If ever a person felt like a ship at sea, it was now, and not simply because of all the naval cant. Cristabel must have been the only one in the house who didn't understand Captain Chase's orders to clear the bridge, scuttle the scuppers, and mizzle the m'nsail—that's what it sounded like, anyway—because the whole staff jumped to battle stations aye-ayeing him to distraction. She understood enough to know she was being hustled out of the house in record time, harp, cash, even a hamper of food from Mrs. Witt. A ship at sea? This was more like a rowboat in an ocean gale with the day's ups and downs, her hopes dashed, her fortunes at low tide, then suddenly riding a crest, and "Clear sailin' ahead," as her companion in the captain's carriage said.

"I'm to be your escort convoy through narrow shoals, miss," he told her, climbing into the coach, near terrifying her at first with the hook he wore instead of a hand. "The captain says to see you snugged in safe harbor, ma'am."

A tall woman could not really shrink into the cushioned seats so Cristabel sat up straighter. "And you are . . . ?"

"It's Jonas Sparling at your service, miss. Late of His Majesty's Navy, able-bodied seaman, qualified to hand, reef, and steer. Now the captain's personal man. His valet, you might say."

At least that explained why the captain was unshaven, but not much else about the man. There she was thinking Chase the greatest beast in nature, a totally untrustworthy rakehell; here she was, her safety and comfort seen to, and her future secured by his generosity. She would never trust him, of course, not that she expected to see him again. The man had been as happy to be quits of her as she of him. Still, there was that debt, the hundred pounds. It was more money than she'd ever had at one time, more than she would accumulate in a lifetime at Miss Meadow's. And there was the boardinghouse, which somehow did not have the same sense of obligation about it, as if the captain owed her something for having gambled over her inheritance and for winning. True, she understood about the card game now, yet couldn't dismiss the feeling that real gentlemen did not play ducks and drakes with people's lives. Whatever she felt, it was done, finished. Chase had invested a great deal in Harwood House, it appeared to her, while he didn't even remember he owned the Kensington place. He certainly didn't need the income from it, or the headache of it, and seemed glad to hand the property over to her. Maybe he had a conscience after all.

First, she told herself as the carriage picked its way through the busy streets, she would repay the hundred pounds, then she would see about the value of the house itself. She *would* make it profitable, she just had to. This wasn't part of her wildest imaginings, running a hotel or whatever, but it was a lot better than her choices of a few hours ago. Sullivan Street in Kensington wasn't Harwood House in Mayfair, but it wasn't the stews and kennels of London, either. Cristabel didn't know whether to laugh or to cry, so she blew her nose. Drat this cold and the sooty air that was making her eyes water.

"Here now, belay that!" Watching the changing expressions on Cristabel's face, the grizzled seaman had been wondering at her fortitude. Fragile young thing looked like she'd capsize with the first breeze, and her standing up to the captain like few men would dare, despite the riot and rumpus heard clear across Grosvenor Square, nearly. They surely were amazing creatures, females, all pluck and backbone one minute, all watery-eyed weakness the next. It was a shame the captain hadn't seen those blue eyes for himself. The color of sunlight on the South Sea, they were. Wellaway, he'd of given her the house and all. Meantime, what did an old tar know about weepy women? Jonas Sparling knew he'd sooner face a boarding party of cutthroat privateers.

"You're already through the shallow waters, miss. No need to fret now. 'Sides, if you can face the captain, you can face anything."

Cristabel smiled at that. "He is rather . . . ah, formidable, isn't he?"

"Aye, he is that. Of course, he's not used to having his ways crossed. In the Navy, you know, captain's word is law. You'd have been flogged, argufying an officer like that."

"Never say so! Not even Captain Chase could be so brutal!"

"Well, there's the conscript, and them taking convicts on as hands; there'd be trouble on a ship lacking some sort of discipline. Skipper might make an example, say, of some young'n who doesn't sing his favorite hymn on a Sunday . . ."

"Mr. Sparling, I do believe you are roasting me."

"Aye, Captain Chase is the fairest man in the Navy, or

was, at any rate. Right now he's just blue-deviled, is all, aworrying about his eyes and if he'll be blind for good and all."

"I didn't know."

"Of course not, and he'd never say it outright. He's just testy, you might say."

"*I'd* say he was a foul-tempered, loud-mouthed brute, but I see by your smile you wouldn't agree. I cannot imagine what the man does to inspire such loyalty. Even Mrs. Witt was singing his praises and making excuses for him."

"Well, I served under him for a good many years, even afore he made captain, and there's no man in the Navy I'd rather sail with. There's no one braver or more generous."

Cristabel made sure her reticule's strings were tightened securely around the precious bank notes. "Yes, it seems I owe him a great deal of money."

"Begging your pardon, miss, I owe him my life."

Miss Swann's settling back on the squabs was all the encouragement Sparling required. There was a ways to go to Kensington, and a tale to tell about all the raging battles, the Azores, and Trafalgar against the whole French fleet, and then *Invicta*'s final battle. While she was engaged with one enemy warship, another loomed up in the fog to *Invicta*'s stern. *Invicta* fired all she could, broadside, before making a run to come about on the other ship aft. The cannon had to be re-aimed and recharged, though.

"And then? And then?"

"And then the first ship caught fire. You should have heard our men shout when they saw the flames and them frogs jumping overboard. And the cap'n, he stands there at the bridge telling the hands steady on, we'd another minnow to land afore supper."

"And did you? Did you sink two ships at once?"

"Aye. And the men were cheering and laughing and dancing about. . . . They were dancing." Sparling's voice faded in the memory until he remembered his audience.

"There was a third ship. The *Ducharde,* damn her. Excuse me, ma'am. We never saw her in the smoke and fog, we only heard the cannon. They hit the ammunition stores. Then there were explosions I never saw the like of, and pieces of ship flying all over, and the men . . ."

"And your hand?"

"Aye. The next thing I know, I'm in the water, and I can't swim. But there's the captain, who's got a great gash on his head, and blood pouring all over his face. He holds me up till we spot a floating hatch cover."

Cristabel let out her breath. "I can see where you would be loyal to him."

"There's more. The *Ducharde* cruised close, mayhap thinking we were Frenchies. They would have left any English sailors, but they recognized the captain's uniform and picked us up. I would have died there again, but for his knowing what to do about the bleeding and all. The Frenchies tossed us in the brig and never looked at us, till they transferred us to a floating garrison. We stayed there for months, rotting, while the Admiralty dickered for Captain Chase's release. I don't know what they traded, but he made me part of the deal, said he needed me. He was in a bad way by then, too, with no proper medical care, so they let me go, to make sure he got back to England. I'd not have made it to the truce, else.

"Now I've got the softest berth of my life, so I suppose I can put up with his shouting a bit."

"A bit? He was very loud."

Sparling chuckled. "Captains have to be heard, don't

you know, even when there's wind raging and surf pounding, and sails flapping."

"Oh, you'd defend him against any charge. Did you hear that there was a . . . a woman," she said, blushing, "in the house this afternoon?"

"Ma'am, everyone in all of Mayfair heard that there was a woman there this afternoon."

Could she blush more? No, it was the fever again. "But . . . but in the afternoon, and in the front parlor, and on the floor!"

"You didn't hear the woman complaining, did you?"

Cristabel knew Jonas was laughing at her, and at this highly improper conversation. A lady shouldn't know about such things, much less talk about them. She hurried to change the topic. "Very well, you won't speak ill of him, but even you cannot condone such wicked gambling."

"No, ma'am, except it did win you this house in Kensington we're aiming at. Pardon me for saying so, but without it you'd be shark-bait, make no mistake."

That was close enough to the truth to give Cristabel pause. "Still," she said, "it's not right."

"I'm naught but an old tar on permanent shore leave, miss. Who am I to say what's right?"

If that were a gentle reminder that provincial, penniless school mistresses had no truck with London ways, Cristabel ignored the hint. The coach was slowing down so the driver could ask directions, and she looked around eagerly. They had long since left the narrow streets of the city which were congested with traffic, noisy vendors, and harassed pedestrians. These roads were wider, tree-lined, and almost empty of carriages. Some streets had attached houses, like rows of uniformed schoolgirls in their church pews. Other wider avenues held modest homes with neat little patches of lawn in front and coach-wide alleys between. Four or five of these buildings could fit on the grounds of the Grosvenor Square properties, but these houses looked comfortable, and comforting to Miss Swann. Tidy and unassuming, they had as little to do with extravagance and wild ways as Cristabel herself. If Fate hadn't been kind, at least she'd been wise.

Fate could have been a little more choosy, Cristabel decided when the carriage pulled to a stop. Fifteen Sullivan Street was narrower than its neighbors, closer to the road, and its tiny front yard was a mud swamp instead of a lawn. The windows were grimy, the steps were hidden under layers of dirt, and the whole house was smudge-colored. No wonder the place wasn't bringing in more income. No wonder the captain didn't want it.

Jonas Sparling cleared his throat. The footman had been holding the coach door open, waiting to hand her down. "Steady on, miss. Take heavy weather bow-on."

She still made no move. "I'm afraid I don't understand, Mr. Sparling."

"Chin up," he interpreted, smiling his encouragement.

"Yes, you are quite right," Cristabel responded, indeed firming her backbone and her resolution. "I have been enough of a ninnyhammer for today. Time to, ah, raise the colors?"

"That's it, ma'am. You'll do. The lad and I will bring in the baggage; you go on ahead."

Her skirts may have hidden wobbly knees, but her shoulders were straight as she walked to yet another new door. Instead of the Harwood crest nearby this one had a tattered, hand-lettered ROOMS sign in a window alongside. Cristabel's knock was just as firm.

The man who opened the door was short and dark. His hair was spiky and he looked up at Cristabel from under bristly overhanging brows. His nose was squashed flat at the bridge, and a damp, chewed cigar stuck out of his mouth. His jacket was rumpled, his open shirt showing a ring of grime on the once-white collar. He was certainly not the type Miss Swann wished to see at her residence. The feeling was mutual. After an insolent perusal of the tall, thin, drab female on the doorstep, the small man announced "You ain't our sort," and shut the door in her face.

What a way to attract boarders! Miss Swann knocked again. This time he opened the door with a grin, not much more appealing with its blackened teeth. "Persistent wench, I'll give you that. You'll have to show me more'n that though."

"I'll show you the door, my man," Cristabel answered, glowering down at him from her seven or eight inch advantage. "I suggest you learn some manners if you wish to keep your position here, whatever that may be. Doorman, I suppose. You'll have to get a proper uniform and maintain a neat appearance. If possible," she added doubtfully.

"Who the bleedin' 'ell do you think you are, comin' 'ere 'n tellin' Nick Blass 'ow to go on 'n what to wear?"

"I am Miss Cristabel Swann, Lord Harwood's niece, and I am the new proprietor of this establishment."

"Like 'ell you are. 'Is lordship's gone 'n stuck 'is spoon in the wall, all right, but 'e never left you in charge 'ere. 'E never even mentioned the likes of no scarecrow niece, so you get yourself back to your blasted convent or whatever, or by God I'll—"

By now Cristabel had heard more curse words in this one day than she'd heard in her whole life, and she was tired of it. Obviously this Nick Blass had never had his mouth washed with soap, like the littlest girls at Miss

Meadow's did, for the merest hint of blasphemy. She doubted he'd had *anything* washed with soap in weeks. No matter what, she hadn't been cowed by the belligerent, bellowing sea captain; she certainly wasn't going to be intimidated by this beetle-browed runt. Little men were often bullies, her father had said, trying to make up in bluster what they lacked in inches. Her pious father was trying to make her more charitable toward one of his congregants, the one who chased the village children with a broom when their balls fell in his yard. Reverend Swann had taught his daughter to be more understanding of men's foibles, so she supposed she'd have to give this Nick Blass another chance.

She pushed past the doorway and told him, "I am not going anywhere, but you may leave anytime you don't like the way things are going to be run here—respectably and respectfully. I'll hear no more of that foul language."

"Why, you—" The furtherance of Cristabel's education in gutter talk was halted by an arm around Blass's throat. An arm which ended in a wicked hook lying alongside his face.

"Avast, mate. You heard the lady." Blass avasted. He stemmed the spew of words to struggle against the larger man's restraint. Sparling was bigger and stronger, but Blass fought dirtier. He bit the sailor's wrist. Sparling loosened his grip, drawing his other arm back for a leveling blow, while Blass reached for his boot and the knife hidden there. Cristabel picked up the first thing she spotted, an umbrella stand. She emptied the contents on the floor and made ready to throw, when a new voice, soft and cultured, neither shouting nor cursing, called a halt to the melee.

The two combatants moved apart, and Cristabel lowered the umbrella stand—an elephant's foot, now that she had time to notice, and shudder. They all turned to watch a blond-haired gentleman slowly descend the stairway, leaning slightly on a cane. Now here was Cristabel's image of a London beau! Muscular physique carefully encased in a close-fitted light blue jacket and buff trousers tucked into gleaming top boots, he had a pleasant smile on his handsome, not-quite-youthful, clean-shaven face. Even his manners bespoke the courtliness of a Minerva Press hero.

"My dear Miss Swann," he said, bowing over her hand (after surreptitiously kicking aside a stray umbrella or two). "I couldn't help overhearing your conversation, and I beg to be of assistance. Major Lyle MacDermott at your service." He even clicked his heels together and flashed her a wide grin, showing sparkling white teeth and a dimple in each cheek. What a sight for a maiden's eyes, especially after the day she'd had.

"For you must know, ma'am, that your uncle trusted me to see to the smooth workings of things here." He coughed deprecatingly, self-consciously tapping his injured leg with the cane. "The baron took pity on a wounded soldier, and kindly allowed me to reside here until I rejoin my unit. I pay a reduced rate, you see, in exchange for my, ah, managerial expertise. Very generous of the baron. I'm sure we all miss him and sympathize with you on your loss."

Cristabel blinked. Generous? Kind? Her uncle? How charming of the man to see the good qualities in everyone. Her father would have approved. Even now the major was recommending that creature Nick Blass to her.

"You wouldn't want to dismiss him out of hand, Miss Swann, even though he's a bit rough around the edges. Not used to ladies, you know. But he's a handy chap, for all that, and you wouldn't want to have to find a man-of-all-work first thing, now would you?"

Cristabel supposed not, even though the little man was glowering up at her still, making her feel soiled. She had never seen Captain Chase's eyes, of course, but couldn't imagine even that raving gentleman's stare holding so much malevolence. She looked away uncomfortably. "He may stay for now," she conceded, winning her another of those heart-stopping smiles.

"Good, good. Nick, why don't you bring in Miss Swann's bags for now while we see what's to be done?" Blass grunted, but he did go out to the carriage. Major MacDermott seemed to notice Jonas Sparling for the first time and dismissed him, too, with a coin quietly pressed into his hand. "I'll see to the lady from now on, my good man," the major said, leading Cristabel away from the hallway.

She would have followed him anywhere, much less into the drawing room he suggested, where they might pursue the discussion more comfortably. She did remember to thank Jonas for his escort, nodding back to his doubtful looks. "I'll be fine now." Of course she would, now that Major MacDermott was on the scene. He was a true gentleman and an officer, treating her with instant respect. Of course, she couldn't quite like being alone with him in the parlor, which was a bit garish for her tastes, but this was no time for lofty principles. She'd already had to overcome a great many of Miss Meadow's teachings on her journey to London and supposed she would have to establish other rules of conduct more in keeping with her new role as landlady. She hadn't given a second's thought to being alone in her uncle's—Captain Chase's house. She had better get used to being unchaperoned in her own house! Major Lyle MacDermott, she was sure, would never go beyond the line, so she was able to wave good-bye to the sailor with all the cheerful confidence, it seemed to that worthy, of a lamb being led to the butcher block.

There was nothing for Jonas to do but leave, however, so he went, scratching his head with the metal crook. He did manage to kick an umbrella or two into that shrimp's path, as Blass struggled up the stairs with the harp.

Back on the street, Sparling gave a last look toward the house before getting into the carriage. Framed in an upper window, waving and winking at him, was a woman dressed only in her underpinnings, from what the old mariner knew of such things, and her ballast was well nigh overboard. If that wasn't one of Mother Carey's chickens, he didn't know port from starboard. This was not a trim rig!

Decidedly concerned, for he liked the game lass, Sparling tried his best to inform Captain Chase that all was not shipshape and Bristol fashion over in Kensington. The captain wasn't interested as he tried to find a comfortable position among the pillows.

"If you delivered her there, and there was a roof over her head, that's all I need to know."

"Aye, Skipper, but Miss Swann—"

"Lord, that woman gives me a headache! I don't ever want to see her again. I don't even want to hear her name again and that's an order. Am I understood?"

"Aye, sir, I ken, but we're not in the Navy anymore."

"No, more's the luck. They don't let females aboard ships there. Now I know why."

Jonas tried again to tell his master that Miss Swann was just a babe. "She don't know—"

"Please, Jonas, please don't talk to me of that shrew. If

not on my orders, then for my peace of mind!" He tried rubbing his aching temples through the bandages.

Sparling gave up in the face of his master's distress. "Aye," he yielded, pouring out a dose of laudanum to ease the captain's pain.

"A promise?"

"Aye, if it'll help you rest."

Chapter Six

"A-achoo!"

"Are you all right, ma'am?" Major MacDermott was all solicitude, offering her a snowy handkerchief. "You seem a trifle under the weather, if you'll pardon my saying so."

Cristabel snuffled. "Thank you, it's merely a head cold," she tried to tell him, but her voice came out a squawk.

He poured a glass of something from a decanter on a side table and pressed it into her hand. "Here, this should have you feeling more the thing."

Cristabel accepted thankfully and gulped it down—anything for her burning throat—and immediately choked on the fiery liquid.

"I am so sorry, Miss Swann. I should never have offered you spirits. I don't know what I was thinking of. Perhaps some tea?"

"There is some lemonade in the hamper Mrs Witt fixed for me," she managed to croak. "Would you be so kind as to fetch it?"

While the handsome officer hurried to do her bidding, Cristabel took a deep breath and a better look at her surroundings. The damask cabbage roses were not to her taste nor the maroon hangings nor the gold tassels decorating the lamp shades, the drapery valances, and the loose pillows. There were an awful lot of loose cushions. Cristabel shrugged. There were no nasty little girls to get into pillow fights here, thank goodness, but there was an old pianoforte shoved into a corner. The furnishings were no matter, anyway, it was the smell of the place that was tickling her throat and making her eyes water. Perfume, smoke, the spirits she'd just spattered, something else even more unfamiliar—

"What is this room used for?" she asked Major Mac-Dermott when he'd returned with the hamper. She was busy finding the jar wrapped in damp cloths and looking around for a glass. She decided to reuse the glass the liquor had been in, so missed the major's wide-eyed start and his creative pause.

"This room? Of course, ah, this room. Yes, why this is where the, ah, boarders can entertain guests."

"Of course, how foolish of me. One cannot expect the boarders to meet callers in their bedrooms, certainly, or transact business matters—Oh dear, don't tell me you have caught my cold already? Here, have some of this lemonade, it's just the thing for coughs."

The major waved away her offer. "Too kind. I'll just help myself to something from the tray here. You did say you were Lord Harwood's niece, didn't you?" he asked while he poured.

"His niece, yes. Uncle Charles was Papa's older brother. My father was vicar to a small church near Bath, however, and they weren't close," she explained, thinking he had noticed her lack of mourning. Her everyday clothes were somber enough to attend graveside services, if she'd considered, but her conscience wouldn't let her forget the lapse in conduct.

MacDermott never got past "vicar" and "church." He

downed another glass. "And you say your uncle bequeathed you *this* place?"

Now Cristabel didn't want to lie to this attractive new acquaintance. Nor did she want to admit to him that her uncle had died a penniless wastrel, leaving nothing to be willed to anyone, if he even remembered that he had kin. It was hard to admit the facts to herself, much less to a warmhearted gentleman who had already professed Lord Harwood to be kind and generous. So she equivocated instead. "The property has been deeded to me, yes. The solicitors are drawing up the papers."

"Strange, I heard something about a young nobleman winning everything off the old bas—baron."

"That would be Captain Chase," she supplied. He hadn't seemed like much of a nobleman to her, or even a gentleman. Of course, Uncle Charles had a title, too, which just went to show. "The captain has taken possession of Harwood House," was all she was willing to say about the situation, leaving MacDermott to infer a great deal more. Before the major could ask any more questions, Cristabel requested that tea he'd mentioned earlier. "The lemonade seems to have given me a chill."

MacDermott hastily glanced at his watch, then gave her a closer look. "Forgive me for saying so, Miss Swann, but I think you'd do better to find your bed, rather than the tea. Colds have a way of settling into one's chest if not cared for, you know. Or the ague."

"I'm afraid you are correct, and I have kept you overlong, besides. You were on your way out when I arrived, weren't you? If you could just direct me . . . ?"

"Of course, my dear Miss Swann. I'll fetch you a hackney directly," he said on his way out. "Which hotel are you putting up at?"

"Hotel? I'm staying here, of course."

The major did an about-face that would have made a drill sergeant weep. "*Here?* I mean here?"

"Naturally. Why ever would you think otherwise?"

MacDermott gasped. "Why ever? Um, ah, because this is no place for a lady? That's it, not suitable at all for one of your refinement and grace."

"Thank you, Major, but I assure you I am not too proud to live in hired rooms. I've been in much worse. Hotels do not treat single ladies very well either, you know."

"No, no, you don't understand," he sputtered. "The other, ah, boarders. They're not at all what you're accustomed to."

Cristabel pictured the quarrelsome chits at Miss Meadow's academy and was thankful. "Really, Major, your concern is touching, but—"

"Working girls—Oh Lord. Shop girls, that's it. And their clients, uh, callers . . . not the type a lady like you should rub shoulders with. Not at all the thing, ma'am, for a real lady."

"Major," she said, "I'm afraid I'll have to learn to be something less than a lady." Cristabel was wadding the handkerchief in her lap so she didn't see how MacDermott's whole face brightened at her softly spoken words, or how his hopes dimmed with her next: "In the eyes of the world, of course. I shall always be a lady in my own estimation."

"And . . . and in mine, Miss Swann," he solemnly vowed.

"Thank you. Now I must trouble you to show me a room. Any clean bed will do. We'll make other arrangements tomorrow, but for now I just want to rest my head."

"No. Impossible. There are no rooms. None at all."

"But I saw the sign . . ."

"Old Blass never takes it down. I'll talk to him in the morning."

"I'll have a deal to say to Mr. Blass in the morning myself. In the meantime I suppose I can sleep on the sofa here. At least there are a lot of pillows."

" 'Oly 'ell, Mac, what are we gonna do?"

"Lord, Nick, I have no idea. We've got Lord Farmington's bachelor party on for tonight and a dying nun on the couch. This'll be a rare evening all around."

"I say we kill 'er."

There was a pause. Either Major MacDermott was too shocked at the idea to express his horror, or he needed time to consider it. "No, the solicitors would only pass ownership of the place on to the next in line to inherit," he finally decided. So much for tender sensibilities. "Let me think."

Not being keen on the practice himself, Nick watched the major's brain in action. It seemed to involve trying to tear great clumps of artfully arranged blond curls out of his head while pacing. Nick shrugged and gummed his cigar, but the method was working.

"I know, we'll stick her up on the top floor in one of the attic rooms. She'll be out of the way for tonight, won't hear a thing up there, and she'll have such a disgust for the place she'll be gone tomorrow."

"What makes you think she'll go for it? Miss 'igh-'n-mighty who wants me to wear a uniform? Fah! The day Nick Blass puts on a monkey suit for the gentry! Anyway, she ain't gonna take no attic room."

"When I turn her up sweet she will. Did you ever know the MacDermott charm to fail? Talk about uniforms, though, I better go change. Never yet knew a woman who could resist one."

Blass expressed his opinion by spitting tobacco leaves.

"Where the hell is Fanny? I sent her to fetch the cursed tea hours ago. Meantime, Nick, you get everyone off the top floor and tell them to stay behind their doors till we fetch them, for goodness' sake!"

"Be a lot easier to kill 'er."

"And have the magistrates down on us? By Gad, Fanny, where have you been, fixing tea for Princess Charlotte?"

"You said she was a lady, Mac. We couldn't serve her out of a mug, could we? Angel had this pretty cup 'n saucer set, it's a souvenir from Battlesea, she says. Only it had some little paper violets glued in, and the glue— "

"Enough, Fanny! Take it in there and for God's sake, don't say anything!"

"Don't say nothing? What'll I do if she asks a question? I mean, a real lady and all."

MacDermott would be bald soon, at the rate he was tugging. "She's not a real lady, with a title and all," he told the girl, "she's just Harwood's niece."

"Sure," Nick put in, "with the hoity-toity manners of a royal duchess dressed in ragpicker's leavin's."

"Shut up, Nick. Go on in there, Fanny, before the tea gets cold. No, wait! Deuce, you can't let her see you like that!"

He fumbled in his pocket—damn, the woman had his handkerchief He pulled the ends of his cravat out from his embroidered waistcoat, only regretting for a second the hour he'd spent tying the wretched thing. He used the cloth to wipe Fanny's cheeks before sending her into the parlor with a pat to her bottom. Then he wiped his own forehead in relief, leaving a red streak across his face.

* * *

Cristabel must have dreamed she was back at the school, for a young girl of perhaps thirteen or fourteen was standing in front of her. No, none of Miss Meadow's students would dare to have freckles like that. They wouldn't be wearing white blouses that fell off their scrawny shoulders, either.

"I'm Fanny, ma'am, and I brung your tea."

"Thank you. Are you the maid here, Fanny? You seem very young."

"I do some of the work here, miss, cooking and picking up. There's a woman comes in for the cleaning, sometimes, and most of the girls eat out a lot or fetch things in. Mostly I'm the 'prentice, so to speak."

"You're the apprentice *what*?" Cristabel wanted to know, but she only got a giggle in reply. "Well, I need some blankets and some hot water. Do you think you could see to that for me?"

Instead Cristabel got a lecture on possets and poultices and learned more about Fanny's poor pa, who always had a weak chest, except he was killed by a runaway horse and not the congestion at all. Fanny left with more giggles, and a promise to return with her mother's special cure-all.

It worked. Cristabel didn't know whether it was the posset, the hot tea, the rest, or simply the young maid's cheerfulness, but she felt much better. No, she had to be honest with herself. It was the sight of Major Lyle MacDermott in dress uniform that had her off the sofa and agreeing to accompany him to the upper stories, where the redoubtable Nick Blass had discovered an unoccupied bedchamber for her.

"Isn't that a Highlands regiment?" she asked.

The major puffed his chest out a touch more in its scarlet jacket. "Yes, ma'am. And no, I'm no Scotsman, but my father's brother is one of those chieftain things there, and he bought my colors."

Cristabel thought they may as well make a tour of the house on the way, since she was feeling quite chipper, and his kilt swayed with every step. She was pleased to note that the major hadn't been badly crippled by his injury. He walked quite gracefully, without the cane in fact, and she wondered if he danced as well. Some of Lord Wellington's officers were reputed to be the finest dancers in all of England. Now whatever put that wayward thought in her head?

"A tour of the house, you say? I'm sure we could have things more to your liking in a few days. You caught us by surprise, you know. Delightful surprise, of course. Baron Harwood was more in the way of an absentee landlord, though, so things aren't quite ready for regimental inspection, heh, heh."

Cristabel was determined to see her house, and to spend a bit more time admiring the major. She wasn't nodcock enough to be infatuated, she reassured herself. She wasn't a silly schoolgirl, after all, but there was no harm in enjoying the company of the first true gentleman she had met since her father's passing. Especially not if he looked like a storybook hero.

So the tour commenced. The maroon front parlor was for callers. Behind it was a dining room, which was more often used as a second sitting room, since no board was provided to the renters and most of them cooked in their rooms or ate at nearby coffee houses. Humbert's was just at the corner, the major informed her, though Cristabel could no more imagine herself sitting alone in a public restaurant than she could see herself ringing the chimes at Westminster.

The dining table could have seated fourteen or so, if it

hadn't been pushed along the wall to make room for more of the flowered chairs and cushioned lounges. Buffet-style, MacDermott said as they passed through in a rush.

"Please slow down, Major," Cristabel pleaded, smiling. "I'll see the dust and worn spots in the morning light anyway, you know."

"What's that? I didn't—Oh yes, well, I warned you how it would be. I, ah, just hate to see a delicate rose in a chipped glass."

A woman's first compliment should be set to music, especially if she is twenty-four years old and can barely recognize it as such. So what was a little bad housekeeping?

The glow lasted through the next door: Nick Blass's office. It must have been the library before the house was converted to flats, since the bookcases were still there, nearly empty now except for overturned bottles and dishes filled with ashes and cigar butts.

What books remained in the room were used as props for uneven chair legs, painfully reminding Cristabel of the precious volumes she had to leave behind in Bath. How could anyone treat a book with such disdain? At least Blass had enough sense to keep the ledgers on a separate shelf, except for the open one on the desk. Seeing where her eyes wandered, the major quickly shut the ruled pages. "No need to bother with fusty old accounts. Nick and I can tell you the particulars."

"I wouldn't think of imposing on you further, Major, and you mustn't think that I am one of those women with no head for figures. I was a school teacher, you know. I did teach music, but the instructors were all required to be proficient in many skills."

"A schoolmistress, you say? Bla—bless you. Still, there's no need to fill your lovely head with figures. I am certain you will find many better things to do with your time now that you're in London. You'll want to visit the shops, of course. What woman can resist? And you'll want to visit all the historic sights so you can tell your students when you get back. Bath, was it?"

"I shall not be returning to Bath, Major, but yes, the shops do sound inviting." That hundred pounds was like an itch. Uniforms for Blass and Fanny, new hangings for the parlor, a cartload of soap and rags—and that was just to start. There were the famous London booksellers, too, like Hatchard's, and all these empty shelves. "Still, business must come first, so I'll want to look over the books myself, but not tonight, of course."

"Of course."

The connecting door led to Nick Blass's bedroom, which Cristabel insisted on viewing, over the major's protests.

"He is my employee, isn't he? No one could complain of the impropriety in that. It is not as though I were visiting your chamber, sir." Cristabel was mortified to find herself blushing. She hid her face in the hanky and gave the room a most cursory examination. Aside from the prevailing reek of tobacco smoke and the unmade bed, the place was almost neat. Small, but not the rat's nest she'd expected from the gritty little man. They returned through the maroon parlor to the entry hall.

"My suite is on the other side of the stairwell," Mac-Dermott told her. "I think you might take a peek at the sitting room without offending anyone's sense of decorum," he teased, having noticed her blushes. He'd also noted what a difference a little color made toward enlivening her looks.

"It's quite large," she said from the doorway.

"But the bedroom is small. Would you . . . ?"

Cristabel was already back in the hallway. "Those must be the best rooms in the house, Major."

"Oh yes, Lord Harwood was kind enough to make allowances for a half-pay officer. The rooms upstairs are all smaller and less costly, naturally, but the stairs are difficult for me to negotiate." His next step was a faltering one, for emphasis. "I'll manage, though, to show your charming self the way," he said, leaning on his cane.

Nick was standing in the entryway, blowing cigar smoke out the door, when the major asked him to carry Miss Swann's bags. He would have kept chewing on the soggy leaves if not for MacDermott's glare, at which he stubbed the cigar out on the doorpost and put the butt in his pocket. Hoisting Cristabel's portmanteau in one hand and the hamper from Captain Chase's housekeeper in the other, he followed MacDermott's cane-aided progress, grunting. Only Cristabel, coming last, seemed to mind the bags clumping on the stairs and scraping against the wall, and the grunting.

"There used to be four bedroom suites on this level," MacDermott told Cristabel as they paused at the first landing. Blass set the bags down and wiped his face with a checkered cloth. "With sitting rooms and dressing rooms, I understand, but when Lord Harwood decided to change the house from a private dwelling, he made all of the rooms into bedchambers. Some of the larger ones have two tenants, and most of the smaller rooms don't have doors to the corridor. An awkward arrangement."

"It's very quiet." The doors were all closed and no sounds reached the hallway, except Blass's heavy breathing.

"The gir—ah, guests keep pretty much to themselves. They'll be at work, or readying to go, or resting from after. Diligent folks."

"They work at night, too?"

"Yes, yes, didn't I mention that? That's why you wouldn't want a room on this story, if one were vacant, which it isn't. The girls come and go at all hours . . . shop girls, ah, baker's assistants who leave well before dawn, and of course some of them attend concerts or the theater on their days off, so it's quite noisy at times. Not what you'd like, I'm sure."

"Do you think I could see the rooms?"

Blass wheezed, but the major ignored him. "Perhaps Fanny could show you in the morning. It wouldn't be proper for me to knock, you know, in case they might be dressing."

"Oh, of course." She thought she heard Blass murmur a high-pitched "a-course" in echo, but when she turned around he was already hefting the bags for the next flight up.

This time Cristabel followed the officer, who oddly enough was somehow managing without the cane again, even though this second stairwell was uncarpeted and steep. Blass trailed after, puffing. Suddenly Cristabel stopped short, struck with a horrible idea. "There are no actresses or opera dancers here, are there?" she demanded.

The major was dumbfounded, seemingly aghast that she would even know about such women. She did, for they figured prominently in Miss Meadow's precepts. It was squash-faced Blass, bumping into her from behind with the hard-edged hamper, who answered: " 'Eaven forbid."

Cristabel smiled at him. "Quite right. This has to be a respectable place, where gently bred strangers can find a secure welcome."

"Quite," he drawled, nudging her onward with the bag.

The uppermost floor would have been servants' quarters. The hallway was dark and narrow and water-stained from years of unpatched roofs. The room MacDermott opened was small, the single window tiny, the ceiling pitched so that Cristabel, at five-foot-eight, would have bumped her head with alarming frequency.

"See? Isn't it perfect?" MacDermott asked. "We usually rent these rooms to transients, except for young Fanny, whose room is at the end. She goes rent-free, for being maid. The other long-term renters are all downstairs. It would mean a loss of income, of course, if you stay here, but you would have your privacy and peace. Why, you could even use next door as a music room. Nick, put the bags down and go fetch the harp." The major continued after the double thuds and heavy clumpings: "That way you wouldn't have to worry over disturbing the boarders, no matter what time you wanted to practice, and your instrument would be safer here than below, where some of the callers might get rowdy. Besides, you'd be out of the hustle and bustle of the common room. Please don't think me impertinent, ma'am, but it would pain me to see a cultured lady like yourself have to participate in the day-to-day workings of a business establishment."

Cristabel was certain she'd worked harder for Miss Meadow than she would ever have to here, for herself, even if she got down on her knees to scrub the floors. The major's concern was touching, it truly was. Of course, his care would have been more affecting if he'd offered her his own suite, a niggling little voice whispered. There were the stairs, and his injury, though, weren't there? And he *was* a paying customer, wasn't he? He smiled at her in wide-eyed expectation, almost like one of her little schoolgirls hoping for a nod of approval for a difficult piece.

And there came Nick Blass, manhandling her precious harp and muttering words Cristabel was sure weren't meant as anxiety over her well-being. Nick Blass, who was too short to bash his skull on the eaves of the attic room, who had a perfectly lovely set of rooms downstairs, including the abused library, and who, furthermore, worked for her. It may be a comedown for a lady to dirty her hands in business, but there were definite advantages, too! In addition, instead of being a ship at sea, it was time Cristabel became captain of her own fate.

"I am sorry, gentlemen, it won't do. As you say, it would cut into the rental income, which appears to be small enough as is. I'm sure I'll have more suggestions about that tomorrow, after I look over the ledgers. I do intend to deal with matters myself, you see, because this is meant to be my income. I shall have to use the office, therefore, so it's only natural for me to occupy that rear bedroom, too."

Nick had been standing pop-eyed from exertion, mopping sweat off his forehead. At Cristabel's words he found the cigar stub and jammed it into his mouth, chomping it around.

It was Lyle MacDermott who hastened to reply: "You can't have considered, my dear Miss Swann, the noise, the dirt from the street, the . . . the . . ."

"There won't be any dirt in my house," she ordered, glaring at Nick. "The condition of this house is abysmal. I lay the blame at Lord Harwood's door, naturally"—her grimace at Nick belied the words—"but this state is no longer acceptable. Anyone who wishes to remain in my employ had better understand. Is that clear?"

Blass started to growl something around the nub of the cigar, but the major interrupted. "Of course it is. The place needs a woman's touch, after all. Isn't that right, Nick?"

Miss Swann didn't wait for a reply before sailing off down the stairs.

Fanny was enlisted to help the furious Nick move his belongings. Instead of facing those stairs again—or leaving altogether as Cristabel hoped—he'd chosen the pantry area for his bunk, dislodging a shadowy figure identified only as Boy, whose duties seemed to include carrying coal and water, though how only the first item got on him was another mystery. The pantry was below ground with the infrequently used windowless kitchen, so Cristabel still had hopes that the surly, unkempt Blass would choke on his own cigar smoke. Boy seemed happy enough to move upstairs, until Cristabel noted the winks he and the maid Fanny exchanged. His pallet was dragged to beneath the kitchen table for now, and he was drafted to shift Nick's possessions and help clean the two rooms while Fanny changed the bed linens.

Nick's thick-browed scowl chased Cristabel into the parlor where she busied herself unwrapping and polishing the harp. She'd had Boy move it nearer the window, thinking how lovely it would be to play there in the morning's sun and how, if need be, she could give music lessons. She was much too tired to try the pianoforte or to tighten more than a few of the harp's strings. She felt as if her fever had returned in fact, and her throat was burning again from the smells in the room. The first thing she would do in the morning was open all the windows! For now she couldn't wait to put her three books on the shelves, her parents' portraits on the bureau, and her weary head on a soft pillow.

Nick's last load was a carved-wood humidor and one boot. Boy tugged his forelock, and Fanny rambled on about new sheets and more time and maybe a plant or two to brighten things a bit, for her mum always said as how growing things made a place look like home. Except for that pretty plant the cat ate and died.

"Fanny," the major said, returning to the room, "Miss Swann is looking a little peaked again. Perhaps you should make up more of that hot posset for her?"

"Please, Fanny, if you would. That would be just the thing."

"And I'll fetch it upstairs for you myself, Miss Swann."

"How kind you are, Major. I'm sure it will help me sleep better."

The major was sure she'd sleep better, too. He and Nick Blass poured half a bottle of laudanum into the cup.

Chapter Seven

"I'm gonna kill 'er, so help me, I am. 'Cept she'd make me carry 'er bloody 'arp up to the pearly gates for 'er."

"Put a sock on it, Nick, we've got to think."

"Think? Huh! What 'appened the last time you put your brainbox to work? I near broke my back and the broomstick moved in anyways. You got about as much sense as you got stuff on under your kilt. Which, incidentally, I didn't see your stiff-rumped moll aswoonin' over."

"She noticed, all right. She's just too much of a lady to show it."

"Yeah, and you were gonna turn 'er up sweet, with your speechifyin'. Any sweeter 'n she'd 'ave 'ad your rooms 'stead of mine. Which ain't a bad idea."

"Especially if I were in them."

Nick hooted. "You're dicked in the nob, if you think you can get Miss Prunes 'n Prisms into your bed."

"I don't know. Did you see her smile?"

"Yeah, right when she was talkin' about how respectable the place had to be. 'Sides, cold comfort's all you'd get out of that one."

"Maybe," the major said with a grin.

"Maybe? Maybe it'd be like takin' a demmed icicle to your bed. There's nothin' soft or cuddlesome about that witch anywheres. And she's too tall."

"Only for you, my friend. I like looking into a woman's eyes for a change. Miss Swann's are a lovely blue, by the bye. Seriously, Nick, I think she's got possibilities. Put a little meat on her bones, do something with her hair, and I wager she'd pay for the dressing. There's something elegant about her, even in that ugly rig she's got on."

"And I say the mort's got an odd kick to 'er gallop. Looks like a feather could knock 'er over, yet she don't bend an inch. Your attic's to let, Mac, if you think you can bring that one under your thumb. I say we get rid of 'er 'n be done with it afore she gets a better look at the place, or the books."

"I told you, and told you, Nick, you can't just get rid of a lady that easily. She's not some two-bit shab-rag you can toss in the Thames and no one would miss or come looking for. You'd have all of London out searching for her and asking questions."

"Then maybe she could just pass on, natural-like. Maybe 'er 'arp could fall on 'er or somethin'.''

"You'd still have those legal chaps out here, handing the deed to the house to some other relict, or selling the place to pay off more of Harwood's debts. Besides, we haven't considered that the girl's got a guardian. You saw the carriage she drove up in, all the lackeys in uniform."

Blass spit. "Uniforms be damned. That's where she got the idea about makin' me into a blasted servant."

"Stubble it, Nick. What do you consider yourself, anyway, an entrepreneur?"

"Huh?

"A business manager?"

Nick drew himself up as tall as he could. "Well I ain't no doorman, 'n at least I ain't aimin' above my touch, like some folks I could mention."

"Take a damper. We've got to figure this out. I did some checking on this Captain Chase while you were, ah, rearranging the furniture. Seems the fellow's become a naval hero since I met him."

"A real hero," Nick taunted in revenge, "or another park soldier?"

MacDermott ignored the implication. "He's got medals and decorations enough to sink a ship, they say, except the ship is already down, blown clean out of the water. He was one of the only survivors, got chewed up some, too. He's selling out now, the talk goes, to take up the family estates in Staffordshire. Came into the Winstoke title, too, and money."

"Yeah, so what's he got to do with Harwood's niece?"

"No one seemed to know, that's why we've got to move carefully. He got Harwood's place in London, it seems, but not much money out of the card game. He didn't get to collect on the baron's vouchers; the creditors got there ahead of him."

"I ain't cryin' for 'im."

"Right, but what about the girl? The way I see it, there are three possibilities. One is that Winstoke is taking her on as a dependent, in which case she's like family, and you know those nobs when it comes to their women. But he wouldn't have sent her here unchaperoned, even if he didn't know about the place. So the likelier idea is that he knew Kensington, and he's set her up here in keeping. And you know about toffs and the women under their protection."

"Yeah, they get tired of 'em fast. This one even faster."

"Correct. And he might just come down hard in appreciation, if we can take her off his hands when the time is right."

"I don't know, Mac. She don't look like no well-kept

mistress to me, an' she sure don't act like any light-o'-love."

"That's why my third theory is looking better, that she really is a schoolmarm who got Harwood's money. I mean, maybe there was something else beside the house the cent-per-centers couldn't touch, entailed jewelry or whatever? Maybe old Harwood settled an annuity on her before he ran up all the debts. I don't know, maybe he even put aside a dowry for her somewhere."

"Lookin' prettier all the time, ain't she?"

MacDermott grinned. "I can't say as how I'd turn my back on the package. A dowry, the deed to the house, and the lady herself. No, a fellow could think of worse fates."

Nick could. He could think of MacDermott set in a soft bed for life, and himself down in the kitchen with the cats and rats, if not out in the cold. "So we got options," he agreed, not mentioning the few he'd keep under his hat for now. "And we got 'er tucked up and out of the way for tonight, but what are we gonna do about business?"

"How much laudanum do you have?"

After five days of rest Cristabel's cold was nearly gone. She had slept enough to make up for those seven years of young girls coughing, whispering, and weeping all night at Miss Meadow's, and the early-morning wake-ups. Now she slept so heavily, it was hard to get up in the morning at all. Staying abed till near noon, when Fanny brought her chocolate and rolls and Boy came in to relight the fire, was entirely unlike her, and Miss Swann reveled in it! She would bathe in a tub placed near the fireplace, then dress and sit in the library reading, or in the parlor playing her music or visiting with whichever of the boarders could spare time to keep her company, mostly a young woman of about Cristabel's age named Marie, who brought in her sewing. Of course, the major frequently entertained her with tales of his travels and a gentle flirtation.

Cristabel's days were delightfully lazy, with only the tiniest twang of conscience to remind her that she was accomplishing nothing. Not refurbishing the house or checking the books or advertising for music students. Well, she hadn't had a vacation in all those years, she rationalized, and she was sick. Actually, she was thriving. With all the care and attention, the good food and even affection, Miss Swann had never felt better. If it hadn't been for the occasional headaches, and worse, the nightmares, she would be like a cat in the cream. For if her days were pleasant, they were also short.

Soon after supper, it seemed, she could barely keep her eyes open. The major had made an evening ritual out of taking tea with her and it was he, to Cristabel's chagrin, who had to lead her, yawning and nodding, back to her chambers. As soon as she had changed into her worn flannel nightgown and tossed some water on her face, she would collapse on the bed. Then the dreams would start.

All those girls—seven years of sweet, laughing little girls turning into hard-eyed predators—ringed her bed, laughing at her. Now their faces were rouged, like dolls, and their laughter was raucous. "You'll never be one of us," they taunted, and only shrieked louder when Cristabel tried to tell them she never wanted to be.

Miss Meadow was there, too. She kept repeating: "You're a bad example. A bad image for the school. Bad. Bad. Bad." Then she turned into Nick Blass, with his broken nose, and he was blowing that rancid smoke at her, yelling, "Bad for business. Bad."

Next the smoke wrapped around Nick's head and

changed into bandages, like Captain Chase's, or like a ghost's shroud. "Ba-a-a-d-d," Uncle Charles wailed, looming over her bed.

Even when Cristabel thought she jumped awake, gasping, she would still hear the loud laughter and her students thumping out tunes on the pianoforte. "Too fast," she tried to tell them, "too loud," but they never listened as she huddled into her covers and fell back to her troubled sleep.

Fanny wanted to call a physician. "It ain't healthy to sleep and not rest. Why, you wake up more tired than you went to bed. Maybe he'll come bleed you and get rid of the restless humors, my mum used to call them. Of course there was Aunt Hattie, who kept her own leeches, all in a jar. Talk about nightmares! She used to say those leeches could cure anything, even the bad head she'd get from drinking too much of her own chortleberry wine. So she'd get herself foxed and spread those leeches around."

"Fanny, no!"

"She did, truly, Miss Cristabel. Only one night she was so jug-bit she forgot to take them off, and they found her next morning, stiff as a carp. And white. Of course, she may of froze to death, being too drunk to light the fire."

"Now I'll have bad dreams for sure! No, I think I just need more fresh air and exercise. I'm not used to lying abed, you know."

"You don't want to go out today, not with that raw wind. Why, I had a cousin Jeb, my mum's cousin what were, and he . . ."

Fanny's artless tales about her enormous family did a lot to cheer Cristabel, who found them especially intriguing since she had no relations of her own. Fanny was content to chatter on with only the slightest encouragement, to relate her kinfolks' varied gory ends, until she remem-

bered her self-appointed task and ran off to fetch a rasp-
berry tart from the bakery, or a meat pastry from the
butcher's boy, passing in his cart. Anything to tempt Miss
Cristabel's appetite. Cristabel had won the younger girl's
instant loyalty by promising an increase in wages, for all
the extra work, as soon as she had a chance to review her
resources. In the meantime there was a gold coin, and the
offer of reading lessons.

"Won't my mum be proud if I can send her some
money in a letter!" Fanny exulted. "Of course, Mum
couldn't read it, but the vicar could tell her what I wrote.
Too bad Uncle Hiram ain't around anymore. He was
book-taught at a charity school once, and they say he was
even reading a newspaper when the house caught fire."

Boy was another new source of pleasure for Cristabel,
although he was as different from Fanny as chalk from
cheese. The lad was shy and untalkative, while Fanny
was a prattlebox; he was born and bred in London, where
Fanny was a transplanted farmgirl; and his family
was . . . small.

"Do you have any brothers or sisters, Boy?" Cristabel
asked one morning while he was carrying in her bathtub,
hoping to win his confidence enough to suggest he use it,
without hurting his pride. Mostly she was curious what
their names would be.

"Yes'm." It was a start.

"Which, then?"

"Two brothers. One sister."

"How lucky for you! I never had any. What are they
called?"

"Son's older. Junior's younger."

"I, ah, see. And your sister?" she asked, hating herself
for such a dumb question.

"Jane Ellen Maria Cassandra Ann."

"My goodness. And what do you call her?"

"Sister."

"Oh."

Boy's family was "gone," according to him. Cristabel didn't probe any further, fearing the worst and not wanting to remind the lad of any sadness. According to Fanny, however, the family had emigrated, involuntarily.

"Pickpocketing. They left Boy behind because he was too slow."

Cristabel did not ask whether he was too slow for the boat or the family business.

For all his reticence, Boy always had a smile for her, under the grime. And he cared about her, too, even before she asked if he wanted to join Fanny's lessons. When he heard about her nightmares, he brought her a gift wrapped in a rag, or his second shirt; it was hard to tell which.

"Bein' alone's scary," he told her as she unwrapped the parcel, gingerly. Inside was a scrap of a kitten of that color cats come in when they don't know who their father is. This one was particularly unappealing, or attractive, depending on one's viewpoint, with a bent ear, a nose that couldn't decide between being pink or black, and a tail like a wet snake.

That night Cristabel's bogeys had orange-yellow eyes and kept pinching at her. The next morning she was covered in flea bites, and the kitten went back to the kitchen, "because he missed his family too much."

On her foray to the kitchen she had been appalled to see Boy's straw-filled tick under the table, making a comfortable cushion for a whole pride of scabby, shabby felines. Her mind was just too foggy to undertake bringing the kitchen to order right then, but she added it to her mental list. In the meantime she told Boy to fetch a cot down from the attic floor, for his bed.

"And where do you think a payin' customer is gonna sleep? On the floor?" Nick wanted to know, coming out of the pantry and scratching his back with a soup ladle. "Or ain't we supposed to be interested in makin' money anymore?"

"If you are so interested in the paying customers," she answered sweetly, "perhaps you should give up your bed."

It was a good thing she couldn't hear Nick's muttered reply, for she was trying to avoid confrontations with the little man for the major's sake. She was still uncertain of Nick's precise function at the house, and she wished to postpone serious decisions until her head cleared.

It was also a good thing she didn't return to the kitchen soon, to visit "her" kitten, or she would have seen all the cats ensconced on Boy's new bed, while a mangy, windy old mutt snored on the abandoned straw mattress. She didn't have to venture down the stairs though. Boy brought the scrap cat to her, with devastating regularity.

A more welcome diversion was one of the boarders, Marie. Cristabel hadn't yet learned to put names to faces, for most of the renters breezed past her short stays in the parlor between naps. Some of the women looked away, unsure of their welcomes, others waved cheery hellos or good-byes on their frequent outings. She was neither fish nor fowl to them, Cristabel realized, neither working class nor aristocrat, and most had nothing to say to her despite their similar ages. For her part, they seemed very busy, very gay, if a trifle loud in their manners which must, no doubt, be due to London's freer, more temperate moral climate. She also noticed that they were dressed better than she would have thought possible for shop girls and bakers' assistants, but what did she know of fashion? She knew they were all dressed better than she was!

Marie was different. Her mother was a housekeeper, so she had been raised with the children of a great estate. She was used to the limbo of governesses and companions, and women who were educated beyond their usefulness as maids and dressers. She was polite without being deferent and friendly without being encroaching. She never asked about Cristabel's circumstances, so Miss Swann had to curb her own curiosity, which was hard, since she had little to occupy her at these times between headaches and sleepiness. Marie, on the other hand, was always sewing.

"Are you a seamstress, then?"

"I do piecework. The other girls are always tearing a hem or ripping a flounce. Sometimes I'll copy a gown for them from the fashion plates. It's extra money."

"Do you think you could . . . ? I'd pay you, of course." Cristabel plucked at the brown bombazine dress she wore.

"I was hoping you'd ask! I kept thinking you would feel so much better in brighter colors, but I didn't want to offend, if you were in mourning."

"No, only in what Miss Meadow deemed respectable garb."

"Grain sacks, more like," and they both laughed, the friendship sprouting on the fertile ground of fashion. Marie was running up and down the stairs with ladies' magazines and pattern pieces, swatches of colors and textures to debate and select. She wouldn't hear of Cristabel accompanying her on the shopping expedition once their lists were complete. "What, in this damp? Mac would have my head on a platter." Marie made no comment on Cristabel's pink cheeks, only reassuring her that this was just a preliminary foray to Grafton's, where the quality was high, the prices low.

"As soon as you are up and about, there's the Pantheon Bazaar and the silk warehouses . . . and there are more booteries and corsetieres than you can shake a feather at. Plumasiers too, of course. What we need to do is make you presentable enough to go shopping!"

"I'd be happy just to go for a walk, but Fanny and Mac—Major MacDermott say I mustn't yet."

"They're quite right. You need to be much stronger. Why, you can hardly hold your head up now. You need to loll around eating all the pastries Fanny buys and the bon-bons Mac brings you so I won't have to keep letting out seams later. What's more, no lady of fashion would be caught dead in a gown buttoned up to the throat, and bones aren't what's meant to show in a décolletage."

"Oh, but I couldn't—"

"Why not? You've got the perfect figure for it. Wait till you get out and see what the duchesses and grande dames are wearing. Next to nothing, that's what. You won't be able to tell the titled ladies from the . . . the . . ."

"The fashionably impure? I'm not such a green gudgeon, you know. Such things are talked about, even in Bath." She didn't mention that such women were only mentioned in whispers, behind schoolmistresses' backs. Neither did she see the need to boast that she would recognize a fast woman instantly. Hadn't she just seen that rouged redhead at Harwood House? That entire sequence was too embarrassing to discuss with gentle Marie, who, for all her London sophistication—town bronze, Fanny called it—was too polite to utter the words. It was the whole terrible memory, furthermore, which was most likely causing Cristabel's nightmares!

Marie was just as eager to change the subject. "In the

meantime, why don't you let me and Fanny do something about your hair?"

"My hair?" Cristabel had pulled her hair back into a tight bun at the nape of her neck ever since she stopped wearing it loose. The style was one of dignity, maturity—and boredom, now that she thought about it. A new life, new clothes, new friends. Why not a new hairstyle?

The two girls primped and pulled. They washed her hair with lemon juice and ale, eggs and honey, and made her sit by the fireplace to dry it. Then they started snipping and crimping. Having friends was maybe the best part, Cristabel mused, while she drowsed in the chair.

For all her years at the academy, Cristabel had no friends, not one single soul to care if she even reached London, or to miss her. Oh, the young girls in her room might weep over her leaving—for a day. They were past the age when anyone who was kind to them became a substitute mother, and Cristabel was too young for that role anyway, but they had liked her, she knew. Of course they did, she bought them things! It was one of her discoveries in her first months at Miss Meadow's, that given enough to play with, youngsters would leave her own things alone. Just like puppies. So she brought them the lending library novels and colored chalk and jackstraws, and in return they gave her a modicum of privacy, along with some affection.

If she was being harsh, considering their fondness a shallow, store-bought commodity, it was from experience. She recalled their tender parting gifts, just as she remembered her reign by terror, threatening to cut their eyelashes off while they slept, if they ever dared to blacken them with boot polish again. She also thought back to all the other years of young girls who, once out of her room and her care, found likelier objects of respect, idolizing the older girls and barely acknowledging the music teacher.

Some of the less haughty senior girls could have been her friends, especially when she first came and was near to them in age. To Cristabel, coming from a small country vicarage, however, they seemed to speak a different language. When the girls reviewed the evening lesson with Miss Meadow, memorizing the London patronesses to whom they must be polite, Cristabel could only wonder. "How peculiar," she chided them. "I was taught to be polite to everyone," which earned her a reputation for quixotic notions and fusty opinions. There was nothing she could teach them about drawing room behavior except an étude, so they ignored her.

The other instructors were older, harried, living for their holidays and a nod of approval from the headmistress. Like Miss Meadow, their satisfaction seemed to come with creating another paradigm of British debutante, ready to take her place on the marriage mart for auction to the highest bidder. The voice teacher would be the only one missing Cristabel, she'd bet, if only for all the extra work that would fall on Miss Macklin's shoulders. As for Miss Meadow—

"There, now you can look," Marie told her, interrupting Cristabel's reverie before she could fall into sleep and nightmare.

"Ain't it a treat? I never would have thought it, even with my mum's receipts. One time she did up my sister Bonnie's hair and it all turned green. Before it fell out."

"Fanny, you never tried that out on me!" Cristabel shrieked. Her bun may have been severe, but it was better than being bald!

"Hush, Fanny, go fetch the mirror."

Cristabel could, indeed, have had no hair at all for the

shock of her image. That streaky, stringy hair of hers was suddenly gold but not blonde, honey-colored but not brown, and it fluffed! Little curls actually bounced as she moved her head and tickled the back of her neck. What remained of the despised bun was a seemingly artless twist of curls at the top of her head.

"Won't I seem even taller?" she asked doubtfully.

"You are tall," Marie answered firmly. "And graceful and quite lovely."

"I bet Mac won't even recognize you, Miss Cristabel."

"*I* don't recognize me, Fanny!" she said in amazement.

"Now all it needs is for me to finish the new blue gown and for you to be well enough for an outing. You'll set all of London by its ear. Or maybe one gentleman in particular?" Marie teased.

Marie never liked to talk about her own beau. He was in the country, that was all she said the only time Cristabel asked, and looked too sad for Cristabel to pry further. That didn't stop Marie from bringing blushes to Cristabel's cheeks, though, with her taunts about the handsome Highlander.

Blushes, at her age!

A beau, at her age? Cristabel wasn't sure, which did not stop her from speculating, naturally. Those air castles of her dreams—her much more pleasant waking dreams—were now filled with air babies, two boys in kilts and sidebars, and a blond-haired and dimpled little girl. She was just trying them for size, of course.

There was no denying the major's attentiveness and kindness, however. He was forever popping in with little gifts to cheer her, candy to tempt her appetite, books so she wouldn't struggle with the ledgers before she was recovered, flowers to brighten her rooms. He had a knack for knowing her tastes, finding Miss Austen's latest novel, bringing nosegays of daisies and jonquils instead of more flamboyant bouquets.

"Major" and "miss" soon turned to Lyle and Cristabel; before long he was calling her *ma belle* and then simply Belle. She could not bring herself to call him Mac like everyone else, nor could she deny him the familiarity of the pet name, not when he spoke it with such fondness.

She had a hard time, for that matter, refusing to take tea with him after dinner anymore, fearing it would cost her his company, even though she felt the heaviness on her stomach was contributing to her disturbed sleep. It was a standoff, however, for his company contributed to her sense of well-being. His smiles, gentle flattery, and tender concern added more to her blossoming than any of Fanny's possets. He cared for her!

"But you cannot keep me wrapped in cotton wool, Lyle. There is so much to be done. I thought that if I could get the kitchen in order and hire a cook, the boarders would take their meals here, for an additional fee, of course. And there's the attic floor. If some of the walls were knocked down, it might make a charming suite for a young family. And the yard needs seeing to, now that the weather is turning, and—"

"Hold," he said, so dismayed that she would think of overtaxing herself that he stumbled over his words. "Soon. That is, too soon. Too much, too soon. There's no hurry, and you're not fully recovered and the weather—"

"How kind you are, Lyle, to worry so about me. I really do appreciate your consideration, but I must start doing things."

"Of course you must," he told her, the ready grin returning to his face. "You've been in the house too long, that's all, and I know just the thing. I've been impatient

myself, wanting to be the one to show you your first
glimpse of London and to witness London's first sight of
you." His blue eyes twinkled as she smiled at the implied
compliment, as he'd intended. "You'll set them by the
ears, *ma belle,* see if all the swells in Rotten Row don't
stare."

"They don't really stare, Lyle, do they?"

"Of course they do, that's why they come. You'll see
for yourself, tomorrow afternoon, if it is warm enough.
I'll hire a carriage and we'll ride in the park, maybe even
see Prinny. That'll put roses in your cheeks, my dear."

Needless to say, Cristabel consigned all those lists of
housekeeping chores to a rainy day—and prayed it
wouldn't be tomorrow, please.

"It's been damn near a week, Mac, 'n no one's come
callin' or sendin' a message. Not even a inquiry. And she
ain't sent anyone to post a letter for 'er, neither. What's
that do to your cork-brained theories?"

MacDermott was disarranging his hair again. "Devil if
I know. We cannot keep drugging her either. She's been
tossing blunt around though. Gave Fanny a nice roll for
foodstuffs, and sent Marie off for yard goods and trim-
mings."

"Think she's got a bundle, then? She ain't been to no
bank."

"You'll have to find out. I'm taking her out tomorrow
afternoon. See what you can uncover in her rooms. Look
in those books she brought, and that portmanteau."

"You don't have to spell it out for me, bucko. Mayhap
you'll explain instead about takin' 'er to the park for the
world to see."

"The chit's like a plum ready to fall. I mean to see
whose lap she lands in."

"Yours wouldn't be one of those standin' by, just in case, would it?"

"Perhaps, depending on what you find in her room."

"Mayhaps she keeps 'er blunt 'n important papers on 'er, what then?"

"Then maybe I'll be the one to find them, after all."

Chapter Eight

"It's too low."

"It's fashionable."

"It's indecent!" The dress was exquisite, what there was of it. Cristabel finally had her cornflower blue gown, tied with pink ribbons under the high waist and edged with a band of pink at the hem. Her golden curls peeked out from a chip-straw bonnet tied with matching ribbons, the bow brushing her cheek. The simplicity of the outfit accentuated her height and elegance—and her bosom.

Marie wouldn't heed her complaints, only repeating that the ensemble was modest by the standards of the day, and she'd see for herself as soon as she stopped dithering and joined the major outside.

"What's more," her friend told her, "that scrap of lace you want me to add would only ruin the lines." So Cristabel appealed to Fanny, who was sitting on the floor playing with the kitten, grinning with pride.

"It's all the crack, Miss Cristabel, really it is. It'd be different if you had no shape to mention. Then you'd want to hide what you didn't have, kind of. 'Sides, you'll need a shawl anyway, till you get to the park. You're not going to waste all my hard work by getting another chill. Why, it was my pa's Aunt Cora what moved to Basingstoke who lived through the typhus, only to go"—

snap—"just like that, the day after getting her feet wet in a rain shower."

Cristabel laughed as Marie draped the paisley silk around her shoulders. "I'm sure this will keep me warm and dry," she said, tugging it closer, to Marie's disgust.

Lyle's reaction was all she could have wanted. His mock astonishment, his bow to her beauty and homage to her sparkling blue eyes and creamy skin were just what she needed to insure her happiness. Until she saw all the other women in the open carriage.

"It was such a lovely day, I thought I would give some of the girls a treat. The carriage has lots of room; I hope you don't mind."

"No, of course not," she replied politely, if insincerely, then asked, "Shouldn't they be at work?" How catty she sounded!

"Kitty is between positions, Alice has a free afternoon, Gwen . . ."

At least Marie was correct, her own outfit was nowhere near the most revealing. Still, the day's light dimmed a bit for Cristabel. It was just that these girls, now laughing and making room for her and Lyle, were not her personal favorites, she told herself, not that she wanted to have the handsome major to herself. Sure.

Well, more fool was she for thinking such an engaging man would reserve his admiration just for her. He laughed and joked with the others, complimenting them as extravagantly as he had Cristabel, to their giddy delight and Cristabel's disappointment.

Still, she wouldn't let a little setback ruin her pleasure in the day, the warm sunlight, her new outfit, her top-of-the-trees escort, as Kitty described him. Lyle was wearing that powder blue jacket she'd first seen and yellow pantaloons. He had big silver buttons, a flowered waistcoat, and a ruffled cravat. Complete to a shade, Alice pronounced. Cristabel thought so, too, though she didn't feel it was quite the thing to say. Some of the other jokes and comments seemed a bit warm to Cristabel also, but she put that down to a working class lack of reserve or London's looser ways. Trying not to be judgmental, for this was, after all, their afternoon off, Cristabel settled back in her corner of the carriage and ignored the silly prattle around her in favor of the wider spectacle.

As they neared the park, the roads were crowded, so traffic moved slowly. Cristabel had time to note the variety of vehicles, the dress of the pedestrians. Marie had been right about the scanty gowns: the only thing keeping many of the women warm was their escorts' smiles. She had also been wise in her warning that there was no telling baronesses from bachelor fare.

Those women at the gates of the park, now those— Mac directed her attention to a smart racing curricle with yellow-picked wheels so her suspicions were confirmed. After that, inside the park itself, the lines were more finely drawn and Cristabel needed Kitty to tell her that the lovely woman in the pink-lined carriage, with her companion demurely beside her, was Harriet Wilson, the best known of all of London's demi mondaine. On the other side of the carriage drive, surrounded by a host of admirers, was a young woman at the reins of a dashing phaeton. This female, Kitty pointed out, was none other than Lady Hanneford, darling of the *ton,* crowned the Incomparable of this season's debutantes.

Cristabel might feel her lack of worldly wisdom, but she was saved from appearing a goggle-eyed provincial by her hat's brim, and by the fact that everyone was indeed staring at everyone else. Especially the men.

Cristabel couldn't feel comfortable under the scrutiny,

but the girls would laugh, and Mac often waved back, so it must be acceptable. Cristabel couldn't help smiling herself sometimes, at the beautiful horses with their buckskin-breeched riders, or the mincing dandies with their striped waistcoats and dish-sized buttons.

The women in their sedate broughams or their military-style riding habits were almost as obvious in their inspections of the carriage's occupants as the men, only less friendly, which Cristabel could well understand. If one could not be sure of greeting a high-flyer or a high-stickler, reticence was the safer course. Still, the women had no need to turn away, Cristabel bristled. They wouldn't be contaminated by the mere sight of the lower orders!

The afternoon parade swirled on with Cristabel trying to get a glimpse of Brummell, or the unicorn rig Lyle admired. Instead, she got a headache.

"Do you think we might stop awhile, Major? My head is spinning from the motion."

"*Ma belle,* forgive me! I wasn't thinking! Here you are on your first outing, and I've been so busy catching envious looks I didn't notice you might be tiring. Here, we'll stop by those trees. Perhaps a stroll would do you better."

Mac forgot all about the promised walk, however, for as soon as their carriage came to a halt, a group of scarlet-uniformed riders trotted over. The officers dismounted, then made a game of racing to hand Kitty and Gwen and Alice down, clamoring for introductions. Cristabel didn't trust those restless horses so close, and the officers' greetings seemed overloud. Lyle's friends couldn't be foxed, could they?

"I think I'll sit in the carriage a moment, Lyle, and catch my breath. You go make the introductions."

He raised her hand to his lips before climbing down.

*   *   *

"I tell you, Perry, it's the prettiest sight I've ever seen! England in the springtime, the trees starting to get new leaves, the grass turning that yellow-green of new growth."

"The chits in their skimpy gowns. I don't know why we couldn't take a drive to Richmond, if you were anxious to see the countryside. *This* ain't pretty scenery, Kenley."

"It is to me, Perry, indeed it is."

The new Viscount Winstoke was sitting up in Perry Adler's high-perch phaeton, drinking in all the flavors of Hyde Park like wine. The colors, the movement, the spectacle of the *ton* on the strut, he was drunk with his first sight of the world outside Harwood House in over a month. That he could see at all was cause enough to rejoice, but this, this was the bubbles in the champagne!

Perry would rather have ale. That Corinthian saw a drive in the park as a waste of harnessing his cattle. He'd rather be tooling his high-bred pair on the open road, instead of jobbing at their mouths to keep them at the slow pace of the carriage drive while his friend ogled the ladies.

"Not in the petticoat line, you know."

"I know, Perry. You're the best of good fellows for carting me about. But pull up, do. Look at the vision over there, the one in the carriage near those trees, in the blue gown. Even a dyed-in-the-wool misogynist would have to have his heart melted at such a picture. I bet she has blue eyes, too."

"Haymarket ware," was Perry's succinct reply.

"Never say so. I didn't cut my eye teeth yesterday, you know. That gown, the simple bonnet. No jewelry, either."

"Bound to be," his friend insisted. "She's with Mac-Dermott, ain't she?"

"I thought he joined up with the Highlanders."

"Yes, when his uncle bought his commission, rather than have him bring any more scandals into the family."

"But that doesn't brand her"—nodding at the woman he hadn't taken his eyes off—"as a lightskirt."

"She's not as flashy as MacDermott's usual style, but you can bet she's in his stable, or will be. There's a house of accommodation out in Kensington."

The viscount was disappointed to hear his swan was a soiled dove, which he couldn't deny, seeing MacDermott kiss her hand. Still, the disdain in Perry's voice was surprising. "What's so bad about a bordello? Don't say you've gone Puritan on me! Just think, such places get the muslin trade off the streets. And where else are the ladybirds going to sleep? No respectable place would have them. I know of a rooming house in Kensington, in fact, where the landlady would have a straw damsel drawn and quartered."

"It ain't the house," Perry explained. "It's that dirty dish himself. 'Ma' MacDermott, they call him. I mean, an abyss is one thing, but a gentleman taking a fee for 'making introductions' goes beyond the pale. They're not happy about it at Whitehall either, I hear."

"What, he's still an officer?"

"Not if Wellington has anything to say about it. MacDermott got invalided home, all right, but no one saw him get injured. It wasn't at the front lines, for sure, where his men were cut down without a commanding officer to relay orders. There's even a rumor about whose gun fired the shot into his leg."

"Devil a bit, no wonder you call him a loose screw. I suppose the rich uncle is pleading his case?"

"Wouldn't you, if there was hope he might get shipped back to the front?"

Lord Winstoke gave a last, lingering look at the willowy blonde. "It's a deuced shame, still and all."

"I can drive over if you want," Perry offered, starting his horses.

"No, if I decide to mount a mistress, I won't need any man-milliner to handle the negotiations, nor would I share her with any man who had the price."

Major MacDermott remembered Cristabel's presence when he saw the smart rig turn to come past. "Belle," he called, hurrying back to her side, "look who's coming. It's Viscount Winstoke and Mr. Adler." His shout was louder than necessary, it seemed to Cristabel, who was already a tad miffed at being ignored for so long on this, her special outing; now he was making her the center of more vulgar attention. The two men may have been his close associates, but, really now, the major should have known better. She couldn't help noticing that the men were a great deal more restrained in acknowledging Mac-Dermott's hail. The driver merely flicked his whip; the other, taller gentleman nodded and raised one corner of his mouth.

Something about that sardonic half smile tickled the back of her memory where she couldn't reach. She would remember him now, that was for sure. Mr. Adler's team was a superb pair of matched grays, and both men were dressed to the height of elegance, yet it was the expression on the dark-haired Lord Winstoke's chiseled face that made the lasting impression. He had character, that was it. He had a firm jaw and an assertive nose, and thick black curls tumbling down his forehead. He was handsome in a very different way from Lyle, seasoned, confident, mature—and that smirk had changed to a tender, wistful smile in the moment the carriages passed and he looked directly into her eyes. That was what she would remember most.

Lyle was staring after the carriage and trying very hard not to rumple today's hairstyle, the Windswept. If he were home it would be more like gale-tossed, but for now he had to make do with twirling his cane, which flew out of control and struck one of the high-strung horses. Being pelted in the rump by an object falling out of the sky naturally unnerved the beast, who took to bucking and kicking, which set the officers to running and cursing, and Alice to high-pitched squealing. Which of course set the other horses off, plus one lady's mount on the carriage path, and Kitty, who was looking for a pair of strong arms into which to swoon.

Cristabel fled. Rather than sit high and conspicuous in the midst of a dreadful scene, she scrambled down from the carriage and tried to blend into the shade under the trees. Totally out of patience with Mac now—the name seemed to suit him just fine suddenly—she kept walking.

Proper young ladies do not wander about London by themselves. Cristabel knew that precept well, and ignored it. This was the park, not the city, and her companions were not far away. She'd seen Gwen stroll off with one of the Army men earlier, and no one except Cristabel had looked shocked, so a lot of Miss Meadow's rules must not apply to ladies without a capital *L*. Furthermore, she told herself as she continued on past the trees to a secluded grassy area, schoolmistresses had always been exempt. A student was not allowed to set a dainty little slipper-shod foot outside the academy without a maid— or a teacher!—in attendance. The chances of a servant being delegated to follow an instructor's shabby footsteps were so low as to be laughable.

In fact, Cristabel had to chuckle, picturing Miss Meadow's reaction to the fast London ways. She'd go all pinch-faced and puff-chested, and start gabbling like a chicken with a fox in the henhouse. And it didn't matter! The sun was shining, Cristabel had her house and her harp, and Miss Meadow could go hang! To prove her point, Cristabel took her bonnet off and swung it by its ribbons, lifting her face to the sun and laughing out loud.

Lord Winstoke also wandered away from his friends. Perry had been stopped by two Belcher-tied members of the Four-in-Hand Club to discuss the merits of Lord Shearhaven's racing stables, soon to go on the auction block. The conversation could go on for hours, Kenley knew, tediously detailed, statistically researched, and excruciatingly boring to one who was not horse-mad. He liked horses well enough, and was looking forward to renewing his acquaintance with the breed as soon as his papers were all processed and the investiture was performed. Then he could finally go home and see if an old salt remembered how to sit a horse without embarrassing himself in front of the *ton*. As for driving, he'd had deuced little experience with the sport, with fifteen years at sea. He'd have to learn, but not today.

Today was for seeing: flowers, a child with a spinning hoop, rainbows in puddles—and a wood nymph, fairy dust sparkling sun-gold in her hair and laughter like nectar on her lips.

"Hello, Bluebell," he said softly, not to startle her. "I wish I had a field of daisies for you to dance in, or a coronet of roses for your hair."

"Oh fiddle," was Cristabel's disconcerted reply. She knew she shouldn't have come so far, alone.

" 'Oh fiddle' is it? And here I thought I was being poetical. I thought of Chaucer's 'fair as is the rose in May,' but it's only April, so I had to be original. Shall I simply revert to plebeian flattery? That's a charming bonnet."

Reminded of yet another stricture she'd violated, Miss Swann hastily crammed the bonnet back on her head. Her fingers were too in a flurry to loosen the knot, so she left it drooping under her chin. "Stop it, do," she told the fine-looking lord, thinking he was making fun of her. "There is no need to pour the butter-boat over me."

Here was plain speaking, indeed, thought the viscount, disappointed that the chit should be so businesslike, even though Perry had warned him.

"What, even if it's not Spanish coin I am offering?"

"Thank you," she said, thinking he meant the pretty words, "but we haven't been properly introduced."

Gads, but MacDermott had her well trained. Kenley told himself he should walk away. Love for hire held no attraction for him, offered no lasting fulfillment. Still, there was that innocent gaze, that sweet curving smile and the adorable confusion when he'd caught her unaware. She couldn't be a hardened jade, not yet.

"But you do know who I am, don't you?" He was sure Mac would have counted off his assets and per annums. At her nod he continued. "And you—No." He wouldn't let her speak. "You can be a fairy princess, Bluebell, just for an afternoon, can't you? It is such a lovely day, and I desperately need a little magic."

She should walk away. There was never a silver-tongued devil who meant right by a maiden, she knew that. But there was that slow, tender smile and those direct gray eyes, one brow raised. No, she could see a scar running through the eyebrow, giving him that quizzical look. She took the hand he held out.

"There is a path to the water through here, if I remember correctly. I want to see if the children still sail their paper boats."

"Did you do that, my lord?"

"Every chance I got. What was your childhood's favorite pastime?"

"It wasn't spinning wheat into gold, I am sorry to say."

She went on to tell him about her music—"What, you even practiced without being forced? You really were an angel-child."—and her books. He let her talk, delighted with her cultured accents, her educated intelligence. In turn he spoke of his brother and their games, their ponies and cricket matches. Not one word was wasted on insincere flattery, or coquetry, or in double meanings. But time passed.

"Oh dear, I must go. Mac will be worried."

"Yes, I've kept you longer than . . . Here, let me help you." Her fingers were again working on her bonnet's strings. Bad enough she'd been missing, she could not return to the crowded area looking tousled.

Then his strong hands were at the ribbons at her throat. For a change she had to look up at someone, to watch him frown at the knot in concentration. At this nearness she could see that the scar continued under the curls above his eye, and called herself a widgeon for worrying that he had been hurt, in a duel, likely. He was nothing to her. He was comely and courteous, but he was a viscount. Cristabel was quality come down in the world, just a vicar's daughter fallen on hard times, and harder, into trade. In a world where "in trade" was a short step ahead of "in Purgatory," the two could never mix, so she could never be anything to him.

Then he had the ribbons untangled and he smiled at her while he tied a bow alongside her cheek, his fingers brushing her skin, his gray eyes looking into her blue ones. And then he placed his hands on her face and drew her closer. He kissed her, as slow and sweet as his smile at first. Now she was the enchanted one, mesmerized by a new magic, a new pleasure, as his arms tightened across her back and his kiss intensified and mingled their breaths, their souls.

Ah, how the two of them could mix after all, she thought in a tingling haze. Then he stood back and the haze lifted and Cristabel realized exactly what she was to him: nothing, that he could treat her so! Worse, her lips were still warm and he was still smiling, laughing at her look of outrage. She decided to flee instead of smacking him or making a scene, which would only confirm his low opinion of her. Actually Cristabel's feet made the decision, carrying her back along the path while her mind was torn between anger, shame, and regret. Anger won.

She was no coward, was she? Then why was she running away from an uncomfortable situation again? He was the one at fault, this man she'd never properly met, taking such liberties. How dare he!

"How dare you!" she told him, turning back to see him in the same spot, looking at her curiously. "You, sir, are no gentleman. You are wrong, furthermore, if you think you can take advantage of an unprotected woman. Major MacDermott would call you out if I told him."

Winstoke seemed more amused than concerned. He crossed his arms and drawled, "Would he?"

Well, Cristabel wasn't positive, to be quite honest. Mac had not taken such good care of her reputation this afternoon, and she was not really his responsibility by blood or bond. Could she ask him to risk his life for what was, on reflection, just a kiss? Her first, of course, and a memory to be cherished, but just a stolen kiss when all was said and done. Perhaps she had been somewhat at fault, too. She looked away.

"I shouldn't have stayed with you."

"No, you shouldn't. But it's all right. You can tell Mac that if I decide to hunt in his preserves, I'll pay the woodsman's fee."

"I don't understand."

"No? Do you understand that if you stay here I will kiss you again?"

This time she did run away.

"May I call?" he shouted after her, and the echoes of her "NO!" blended with his laughter.

Chapter Nine

"So Winstoke didn't notice 'er 'ighness at the park. What now?"

"Oh, he noticed her all right, he just didn't *know* her. Did you find anything in her rooms?"

"No papers, no cash. What are we gonna do?"

"Keep writing."

Mac and Nick were busily engaged in a major creative effort: fabricating a new set of ledgers out of whole cloth. They worked with fresh ink, watered ink, seven different quills and two nubby pencils, taking turns with their right hands, then their left hands. They added tea and wine spatters for authenticity, and a boot-heel scuff for good measure. Their minds were so taxed with making up new debits—"Do we *have* fire protection, Nick?"; "Sure, there's a bucket out back."—that it was no wonder they couldn't find a solution to the problem of Miss Swann.

"Business is way off, you know," lamented Nick.

"Why? The gents don't seem to mind using the back door and my sitting room, and the girls are being good about keeping them quiet."

"It's not from missin' the parlor, you nodcock, it's the blasted music comin' out of it. 'Arp playin' don't exactly set the right mood, if you get my drift."

"Well, I don't know what you expect me to do. She

won't take so much as a sip of wine or tea in the evening, and I am already keeping her out of the house as much as possible. We've been to every church and tourist spot and regimental drill. I've taken her to Drury Lane and the opera and even Astley's Amphitheater. Incidentally, you should see the wenches at Astley's in their tights and spangles."

"There's a gaggle of women upstairs. Can't you get your mind off the petticoats 'n back on business?"

"We'll go to Vauxhall come Friday night, all right? I've run through a month's pay already, entertaining her."

"Too bad, so long's you keep 'er out of my sight. I was thinkin' on a more permanent solution 'owsoever."

"I have it in mind, the dibs just haven't been in tune. Have you seen the way she's looking now?"

"Yeah, so she's not something one of Boy's cats drug in. She's still a long Meg."

"You're blind. She's exquisite. You should see the bucks ogling her."

"I've seen you droolin' at 'er. That's enough."

"There's a fortune to be made off her, you just wait and see."

"What about your plan to marry 'er 'n get hold of the deed?"

"Unless she's got a full account somewhere, it won't fadge. *I* can't live on my income, no way it'll cover her, too. No, she'll have to earn her own bread."

"Mac, you're more of a clunch than I made you out to be, 'n that's sayin' a lot. She ain't goin' to tumble, face it."

"She hasn't thrown her bonnet over the windmill yet, I'll grant you, always bringing Fanny or Marie along, but maybe Friday. You know Vauxhall, the lanterns, the music, the fireworks . . . the Dark Walks, heh-heh."

"So she falls for the music 'n your pretty face. You get your itch scratched, what then?"

"Then she won't have much choice. These," he said, tapping the fake ledger books, "will show her she's got no income, so once she's blotted her copybook for good and all . . . Hell, she was ruined the minute she walked into this place, she just doesn't know it yet."

There was a lot Miss Swann did not know. Like how a rooming house could have no vacancies and no money both. Or why Mac was such a restless soul, forever needing to be out and doing things, and surrounding himself with his officer friends other times. Or why the boarders giggled at her, or why Marie's beau would never make an appearance. She was too busy to worry; she would do that next week, when she measured the parlor for new drapes and had the pianoforte tuned. This week was already full with things for which she had been waiting her lifetime; the house could wait a few more days.

How could she concern herself with the condition of the kitchen stove when there were dress fittings with Marie, trips to the parks with Fanny, sight-seeing with Mac, the park, the opera . . . and Lord Winstoke.

For there was one thing Miss Swann knew that Mac didn't: how very close she was to losing her heart, if not her head. But not to him. It seems that a rare smile meant more than a facile grin, a thoughtful discussion more than flirtatious banter, and understated courtesy more than overblown gallantry.

On the days following her first excursion to the park, Cristabel was anxious about leaving the house lest she come face to face with his lordship again. Then she was nervous to stay home, in case he should call. It was only a kiss, she told herself, there was no need to be embarrassed. He would already have forgotten it, a man of the world such as Winstoke. She would forget it, too, see if she wouldn't. So she threw herself into being a tourist and a bargain-hunter, and there he was.

Marie knew all of the best places to purchase gloves and lace and slippers to match the new gown Cristabel would wear to Vauxhall. In this case best meant least expensive, especially once Cristabel realized how far her hundred pounds would have to go before the house made a profit. So it was the Arcade and the Emporium that drew Cristabel's trade, not the exclusive shops in Mayfair, where a single gown would cost her entire fortune, and more. Still, looking was free, and Cristabel had gotten over glancing in every carriage and behind every tree for a tall, dark-haired gentleman. She had even stopped fretting that one of her former pupils would recognize her. None of them had enough intuitive sense, but if they had, Miss Swann refused to be ashamed of her new middle-class respectability.

"Why the frown, pretty Bluebell?" a too well remembered voice was asking. "If you don't like the bonnet, there are hundreds more."

"Oh no, the bonnet is lovely. It was my thoughts that—Whatever are you doing here, my lord?" Cristabel glanced around. Marie was talking to the shop assistant near the display window; the owner was helping two dowagers adjust their turbans. Even if there had been other men in the small shop, she could not imagine anyone appearing more out of place. With his buckskin breeches, shiny top boots, and a dark blue jacket perfectly tailored to accent his broad shoulders and narrow waist, Lord Winstoke looked ridiculous among the feathers and froth. And very appealing.

"Here, try this one," he said, offering her a confection made of stiffened ecru lace and trimmed with silk roses. Cristabel hastily tied the bow herself, remembering his touch last time. She wasn't surprised to find the bonnet was exquisite. Trust a practiced flirt to know all about women's fashions.

Still frowning, which didn't do justice to the hat, she repeated her question. "I doubt a gentleman spends his time in fancy shops, my lord. How did you happen on this one?"

"Oh, I was driving by and saw you enter. Actually, my friend Perry was giving me driving lessons. It seemed better to end the session while we still remained friends. How he expected me to handle his pair in traffic first thing is a mystery. Uncooperative and meddlesome."

"His horses?"

"No, Perry. He's usually the best of fellows, except when it comes to his cattle. I'll use a hired pair from the livery from now on."

"Forgive me for my curiosity, but how does it happen that a gentleman who is so . . . so . . ." She caught herself from borrowing Fanny's phrase about being bang up to the mark. "That is, I thought all gentlemen could drive."

"What, did you think we were born with the knowledge, along with the silver spoons? Don't look daggers at me, I am only teasing. You are right, of course. I would have learned years ago, but for being off at the wars. I don't think that hat will do, after all. It shades your eyes too much."

If he could change the topic quickly, so could she, rather than have him continue this line of talk which was too familiar for her comfort. It was one thing for Marie or the shop girl to offer advice; they didn't stare at her so intensely, starting chills along her spine and fuddling her thoughts. To divert him from his scrutiny, remembering how Mac loved to recount his tales of valor, Cristabel asked if Lord Winstoke had received the scar on his forehead in an act of heroism.

"There were no heroes, ma'am," he answered brusquely, turning away. "Only survivors."

"I . . . I am sorry, my lord, forgive me if I—"

"No, no, it's just me. Besides, I believe I owe you an apology for the other day. I am not sorry, mind. No, that's no way to begin an apology, is it? Miss Belle, I cannot regret the kiss, but I humbly beg your pardon for upsetting you. Am I forgiven?"

Cristabel quickly looked over her shoulders to see if anyone heard. Oh dear, he hadn't forgotten the kiss at all!

"Can we cry *pax*?" he asked, a little louder, causing heads to turn in their direction. The dowagers sniffed, but Marie winked!

"Yes, yes," she cried, to shush him. She hurried to the rows of bonnets on the wall, turning so he wouldn't see her dratted blushes.

He was right behind her, pretending to deliberate over the selections while she pretended her heart wasn't pounding at his nearness.

"At the risk of being indclicate," he said quietly so no one else could hear, "have you found someone to, ah, help with finances?"

Now how could he have known about the harp lessons? Mac, of course. It was just like the rattlepate to broadcast her economic embarrassment. "No, I haven't advertised yet," she answered crossly.

Eve never advertised either, he thought, astounding himself with the relief he felt. The other marvel was that no man had claimed her yet, unless, of course, she was holding out for a higher price. Kenley had tried to put her from his mind, with less success than he'd had driving Perry's horses. Seeing her again, he decided he may as well get her out of his system, especially if he could make an arrangement without having a distasteful conversation to deal with MacDermott. These things never lasted long, at any rate. And in the meantime . . .

"Here," he said, offering what she thought was another hat for her to try.

This one was gorgeous; a tiny scrap of blue satin with a ruched brim, it had two feathers dyed to match, affixed with a lace bow and made to curl down her cheek.

"Perfect," the viscount declared. Even Marie and the salesgirl came to *ooh* and *aah* over her. Cristabel hoped Marie especially was taking careful note of the bonnet so they could copy it, for it really was the most becoming she had seen. Regretfully, she took it off and handed it to the clerk with the age-old excuse: "I'll have to think about it."

"What, you don't mean to have it?" Winstoke protested as he followed her toward the shop's door. "But it was the same color as your eyes."

"Of course I won't buy it," she told him. "It is much too dear." She looked at him puzzledly, wondering how, if he knew about her financial difficulties, he could consider the bonnet within her means.

Ah, that look of inquiry. Winstoke knew his role well, he believed. Without a moment's hesitation he recited his lines, offering to purchase it for her, only to be stopped short with her instantaneous "Certainly not."

"No? You are the only woman of my acquaintance ever to turn down a gift. May I ask why?"

"It wouldn't be proper. A gentleman never buys a lady's clothes, does he?"

There were the occasional dashing widows and straying wives, but "Not a lady's, no," he admitted.

"Well, I *am* a lady, despite my circumstances. Is that perfectly clear?"

With her blue eyes blazing and her posture as rigid as a topgallant mast, she gave a damn fine imitation, Win-

stoke decided. He had no idea what game she was playing now, or what the rules were, but all those years at sea
had taught him patience. The more he saw of Belle, the
more he wanted her, so he would wait.

"Very well, sweetheart, have it your way. May I escort
you and your companion to Gunther's for an ice?"

After that, Winstoke never called her anything but
Miss Belle, or my lady; he never called at Sullivan Street;
and he never tried to kiss her again. He did appear in
Kensington Gardens when Cristabel walked there with
Fanny, choosing the less fashionable grounds instead of
going to Hyde Park with Mac and the girls and the soldiers and the stares. He even showed up at Somerset
House, after she mentioned Lyle's reluctant agreement to
take her to see the art exhibits. The major grew pre-
dictably bored after the third noseless Greek statue, and
stepped outside to blow a cloud. He never noticed when
Cristabel wandered off with Winstoke and Fanny like a
freckled shadow behind them, to view a Turner seascape
the viscount particularly admired.

Naturally she told him they were to attend a performance of *Romeo and Juliet* that night, so she wasn't surprised to see him during the intermission; she was only
surprised he could find her, with the crowds around
Marie, Kitty, and Alice.

Cristabel had been delighted at the prospect of seeing
a play she had only read. Twice yearly Miss Meadow permitted the upper girls to attend a traveling company's
dramatic performance in Bath, well accompanied, of
course. Miss Swann counted herself fortunate when she
was designated among the chaperones, instead of remaining behind to baby-sit the younger girls. Over the
years she had seen several mediocre *Hamlets*, an affecting *Lear*, and an incomprehensible *Henry IV*, among oth-

ers, but never *Romeo and Juliet,* as Miss Meadow considered the tragedy far too suggestive for her tender charges. A particularly bloody *Macbeth* was acceptable; the story of impetuous lovers was not.

The Theatre Royal in London, however, was a totally dissimilar experience from the entertainment in Bath. Here, for instance, the play was followed by a farce so warm Miss Meadow would have lowered her fees before she would let her girls see it. The audience was much more unruly, furthermore, the bucks in the pit booing, throwing things, and shouting so loudly at the stage and each other that Cristabel could barely make out the actors' lines from her seat in the balcony. Not that it mattered. Juliet appeared to be well past her prime, and Romeo was a mincing fop.

"Mac, these seats are lovely, but I was just wondering if the boxes were terribly expensive? I mean, if I should consider taking one for the season, next year."

The major wasn't the slightest bit offended. "Sure, those swells can see and hear everything, can't they, without worrying over the stray orange rind or two. The season costs more than my quarter's income, though, and there is even a committee to approve the box holders.

"That's a pretty lesson for you, my dear," he said, patting her hand. "Being poor just ain't as much fun as being rich."

Cristabel drew her hand out from under his and turned back to the stage. At least the balcony was better than the pit.

The first intermission was unpleasant. Cristabel felt smothered by the press of people. The scarlet uniforms and formal black jackets were exciting to look at, but not when they were shoving and standing too close or spilling glasses of orgeat in their efforts to move through to their seats. Marie was used to it all, laughing and making small talk with the men around them when the major left with Kitty and Alice to fetch drinks. Cristabel stared at the boxes again, discouraging any overfamiliarity from the milling crowd.

Marie suggested they all walk in the lobby during the second break, and that was a little better, until another group of men hailed Mac and surrounded the small party. Cristabel didn't catch any of the names, titles, or ranks, she just nodded unhappily, wishing Romeo and Juliet had never met.

And then Lord Winstoke was there, offering his arm. A path cleared instantly for Cristabel and the imposing viscount, whose single glance kept the other men at a distance. A respectful distance.

"So what do you think of the young lovers, Miss Belle?" he asked, as if he had not found her in an uncomfortable situation, and she was able to laugh at his description of Romeo, checking behind him to see if he had caught his hose on the fake roses, when he'd climbed to his lady-love's balcony.

The opera was an altogether different prospect. A gentleman friend of Kitty's had an aunt who had a box not being used that night. Cristabel switched seats to have one farther back in the shadows, after being ogled before the lights were dimmed. She could still see the opulent surroundings, the lavish gowns and jewels, and the play of people who came more to be seen than to see the performance. Then the opera started and Cristabel was lost.

No amount of noise from the rowdy bucks or gossip from the wasp-tongued matrons could interfere with Miss Swann's pleasure in the music. She didn't even notice the flux of visitors to and from the box at intermission, like changing tides, so rapt was she, playing the chords over in her mind. She did spare a thought for poor Miss Macklin, the voice teacher, for missing such a performance, and the great Catalani was not even singing that night!

She also gave passing consideration to the fact that Kitty and her beau, who seemed to have a title but no chin, did not return to the box after intermission. How sad for Kitty to get the headache and have to miss the rest of the opera.

The box was a great deal quieter after the second act. Coming back from her reverie with a start, Cristabel was shocked to find herself alone in the darkness with a man, until she realized it was the viscount, watching her and watching over her, smiling at her pleasure, sharing her enjoyment. He was dressed superbly, too, with a diamond stickpin reflecting the chandelier's glimmers.

What a heady, magical night for Miss Swann the schoolmistress. There she was at her first opera, a handsome nobleman choosing to sit quietly at her side rather than pay court to society's belles. Imagine what she would have missed if she hadn't come to London!

His lordship was the only thing she missed in all of London over the next few days. Mac seemed determined to introduce her to the city's marvels all at once. St. Paul's, Pall Mall, London Bridge, and the Tower to view the menagerie. Dear Mac even took her to Astley's Amphitheater to see the equestrian acts. Too bad the fancy riding only reminded her of Winstoke and his driving lessons. Too bad that MacDermott's guidebook garrulity made her long for a thoughtful phrase and a companionable quiet. And too bad, especially for Mac's plans, that when Miss Swann dressed for that romantic evening at Vauxhall, she did so with Winstoke on her mind.

Chapter Ten

"Very well, we've been through it before, and I won't add the lace fichu. But Marie, I never wanted to be a . . . a dasher, you know."

No one would know it, to look at the once-demure Miss Swann, dressed for her evening at Vauxhall. Will she or won't she, the retiring, mousy schoolmarm was stunning—and sultry.

Marie had come upon a roll of gold-shot natural silk which had been discolored with a small water stain right through the bolt, so the tradesman was happy to let it go for just pennies a yard. Cristabel and Marie had taken turns embroidering gold-floss butterflies over the blots as they appeared in ordered rows down the front and back panels of the narrow skirt, and another, larger gold butterfly outspread at the décolletage. A few more on the wispy gauze overskirt, and Cristabel's gown appeared held together by gossamer wings. She floated, and the tawny color blended with her skin. A gold satin ribbon wound through the curls piled on her head, leaving a few to trail down one otherwise bare shoulder.

"You just wait till your handsome viscount sees you," Marie teased. "Talk about fireworks!"

Cristabel fussed unnecessarily with a wayward curl. "You know he's not *my* viscount. I have merely walked in the park with him a few times; that doesn't mean anything, not with men of his stamp. He is just being kind." Marie was still grinning, unconvinced. "Very well, he did seek me out at the theater and sit with me at the opera. He finds my company restful, he says. That's all there is to it."

"We'll see how restful he finds you tonight. They say he's—"

"No, I shan't listen to gossip. None of it matters, for he's still way above my touch and we both know it. Furthermore, Mac is my escort this evening."

Marie wrinkled her nose at that. "Mac only thinks he is your escort. You cannot gammon me as easily."

"We'll see. Are you sure you won't change your mind and come with us?"

Now it was Marie's turn to look flustered. "No, I would rather stay at home. I . . . I received a letter today."

"From your beau? How wonderful for you!" Cristabel wouldn't gossip, not even with little Fanny, but she couldn't help knowing that Marie had been concerned with her gentleman friend's absence. There were great expectations from him, it seemed, when he returned. "Is he back in London yet?"

"No, but he wrote that he was starting out."

"And he'll rush over here first thing, I'll wager. Of course you must stay in tonight. I suppose I'll have to reconcile myself to losing you altogether."

"Nothing is certain yet. That is, I do have hopes, but . . ."

"Of course, it wouldn't be proper to speculate further. Oh, I hope he comes back soon. Do you love him very much?"

"Well, he's very handsome, and very rich."

Which answered the question perfectly, to Marie's

thinking, if not Cristabel's, who was afraid her friend was mistaking cream-pot love for something more. Heaven knew, she was no expert on these matters. Just look at the tangle her own heartstrings were in.

"I still wish you were coming along tonight," she said. "I'd feel much better with you there. I am not sure that Vauxhall is quite the thing for a single lady."

"Oh, you'll do fine with Mac, and Kitty's going along, too. Some of the other girls might stop by after the, ah, party they're attending."

"But Kitty's always getting headaches, you know, and leaving early. Don't laugh, she does. And Mac is getting, well, particular in his attentions."

"I'm sorry for making light of your worries, really I am, and I'm certain you'll lower Mac's pretensions in good order. It's just that here you are, a beautiful woman, and you still think like a downtrodden governess."

"I am pretty, aren't I?" Cristabel asked wonderingly. "I knew you and Fanny had done miracles with my hair and my clothes, of course, but I never realized . . ."

"Silly goose. Did you think it was just your conversation the men admired? You could speak Hindustani for all the difference it would make. Half the time you never open your mouth anyway and still have most of the males in London begging Mac for an introduction. Why, I'm hoping you won't be home when Radway calls, else he might forget why he came. Now go and have a good time, and for once, bend a little. No, I don't mean you should slouch! Just enjoy yourself."

She tried, she really did, to savor the gay music and laughter, the twinkling fairy lights strung in the trees, even the shaved ham and arrack punch served in the private boxes. But it was hard to ignore the other side of

Vauxhall: the squeals coming from behind bushes, the roving groups of bucks more than a little well to pass, the noticeable lack of fashionable matrons with their debutantes on exhibit. Although Society's raffish sons frequented the pleasure gardens, Vauxhall was no longer a secure place for its pure daughters. Or for Cristabel Swann.

Kitty got the headache again, and her chinless swain took her home.

Cristabel thought it was a fine excuse and tried it on Mac, but he would have none of it.

"We can't go home so early, *ma belle,* not without seeing the fireworks. We haven't even had a dance yet, and you haven't tasted the syllabub. Here, have another sip of punch. It will take care of your headache in a trice."

The spiced drink was more like to give her a megrim for real, Cristabel decided. She took advantage of Mac's conversation with the party in the booth next to theirs to spill her cup onto the grass beneath the box. Mac filled her glass immediately again when he turned to introduce her. The women's faces were painted, Cristabel would swear to it, even in this uncertain light. For once she was glad of Mac's casual manners.

"Belle, this is Coco. That's Tiffany. Fellow on the ground is Orr, and the chap with the foolish grin is Mr. Smith. Here, let's have a toast. To *amour.* What else in the pleasure gardens?"

Cristabel realized Mac was already foxed, so she spilled out his glass, too, the next time he looked away. He kept refilling them, and she kept emptying them, and the strays and rodents that lived on the crumbs beneath the boxes would all have headaches in the morning.

"Come on, Lyle, why don't we go for a walk?" she suggested. If the motion wouldn't sober him, at least he would be away from the punch bowl, and those dreadful people.

"Sure, I know of the prettiest little bower just a few steps away down that path there."

There were no lights where he was pointing.

"I've changed my mind. What about that dance you promised me?"

If Cristabel had a shilling for every hour she'd spent playing the pianoforte during the students' dancing lessons, she would be wealthy, enough to open her own academy, which nevertheless made her an unpracticed dancer. She had natural grace and music sense, and knew all of the steps, yet she felt clumsy, off-tempo. Mac's lead was awkward, the music was too loud, and the other couples on the planked dance floor were not keeping to their patterns either, bumping into them and laughing uproariously. Soon Cristabel was hot and damp, with aching feet where Mac had danced right on her thin silk slippers, leaving black smudges across the toes.

"Mac, do you think we could take a break? I would dearly love something cool to drink."

"Of course, my love. Let's go back to the box and have the waiter refill the punch bowl."

That was another bad idea. "No, not more of the punch. Some lemonade perhaps? Why don't I wait here while you fetch it, then we can have another dance."

"Fine, fine, whatever you want. Lovely night, isn't it? Maybe they'll play a waltz."

Miss Swann would have the grandfather of all headaches—no, she would have a fainting fit—before she let the major maul her about in the intimate embrace of that dance. Miss Meadow permitted no practice sessions, not even for the senior girls, and only one demonstration, where the pouter-pigeon headmistress herself waltzed with the oily dance instructor. If that wasn't enough to kill any romantic notions the girls may have had about the new dance, nothing would. They'd practice with their brothers, when the Almack's patronesses gave permission.

"Care to dance, lovey?" Mac was nowhere in sight, and an old man in a bagwig was bowing in front of her. She could hear his corsets creak.

"Thank you, no. I am waiting for my companion."

"So, one's as good as t'other. Come on now."

"No, I really prefer to wait for—"

"What's a matter? I'm not good enough for the likes of you? Hah! I'll just show you—" And the aged roué grabbed her arm and started dragging her to the dance floor.

Cristabel struggled to free herself, looking around frantically for Mac. Then suddenly the grip on her arm changed.

"This is my dance, I believe."

She looked up into angry gray eyes and clenched jaw. "L-Lord Winstoke," she stuttered, "how did you— That is, thank you."

"You little fool. What are you doing here by yourself?" He gave her arm a shake.

"Mac went to fetch some lemonade and I didn't know there would be a problem. That man—"

"You should have known, damn you! What did you expect, coming here dressed like that? Good grief, girl, you're enough to drive any man to mayhem. If I weren't a gentleman, I'd drag you down the Dark Walks myself!"

If that was a compliment, it was a long way from warming Miss Swann's heart. "Very well, I have made another foolish error, like wandering off in Hyde Park with a strange gentleman and letting him kiss me. It won't happen again, I assure you."

"Pull in your claws. I know I've no right to lecture you. What could that gudgeon MacDermott be about, to bring you here and then leave you?"

"I intend to find that out myself, my lord. If you would just walk me back to my box . . ."

"Don't you remember? It's my dance."

Of course, it had to be a waltz. And, of course, the viscount danced exquisitely, making even the inexperienced Cristabel feel light as a moonbeam, like a butterfly new out of its cocoon, trying its wings. Miss Meadow, eat your heart out!

No wonder they don't let debutantes waltz, Cristabel considered in a daze. It really was dangerous. She could feel Winstoke's hand strong and confident at her waist through the thin fabric of her gown, and she could breathe the scent of his lemon soap. Most of all, she was close to that softly curling smile, the lips—

"There you are, Belle. I was wondering where you'd got to. I had the devil's own time finding lemonade. Servant, Winstoke. Come along, Belle, the other girls have arrived. They're waiting in the box."

"We haven't finished our dance, my dear," Winstoke said quietly.

Oh, how she wanted to stay in his arms. And what a dangerous mistake that would be, she knew from his narrowed eyes and from her own heart's thudding in her chest.

"I'm sorry, milord. I must return with Major MacDermott. Thank you again."

He bowed over her hand and turned away without another word.

"Bit high in the instep, huh?" Mac remarked. "He didn't, ah, go beyond the line, did he?"

"That's just what I want to discuss with you, Lyle. I think we should go home and have a long talk."

"Fine, fine, long carriage ride and all. I just promised some of the chaps a chance to meet Alice and Gwen and Angel. Only take a minute."

It took a great deal longer, threading their way through the crowds, louder now and more coarse in their comments and gestures. The girls in the box were already sipping their punch and giggling at the usual complement of red-coated officers. One of her least favorite of the boarders, Lucy, who rouged her cheeks, was drinking from a glass held, of all things, by the ancient rake who had accosted Cristabel at the dance area, a Sir Winklesham. Mac was calling to men across the box rows, sending Alice and Gwen off to dance with a stammering baronet and an obese man he whispered to Cristabel was Mr. Frye, a nabob with one of the trading companies.

"They're going in the wrong direction for the dancing, Mac."

"What's that? Oh, they must be going off to watch the fireworks instead. Should be starting soon. We ought to get along, too, to get a good spot for viewing."

"Mac, I am not going anywhere until I have some answers," she hissed. "Get rid of all your friends and for goodness' sake, put down that glass."

"There now, no need to get in a pother. See, everyone's leaving for the entertainment anyway. We can stay right here and have a comfortable coze. I've been meaning to talk to you for some time now anyway."

"You have? I've seen you every day and you've never said anything."

"Always people around and all. But you go first, my love," he offered pleasantly, patting her shoulder.

She cringed, but went on gamely. "Mac, this isn't a proper place for you to bring me. You do know that, don't you?"

He had the grace to look uncomfortable. "I thought you might have a good time, that's all. The other girls never minded."

"That's another thing. You are forever introducing the girls to your friends from the barracks and all those lords and wealthy merchants. But they aren't really interested in poor shop girls, are they? I mean, they'd never marry Kitty or Gwen or Alice, or take Lucy or Angel home to their families, would they? Why don't the girls go out with footmen or clerks or even common soldiers, so they can make respectable marriages?"

"Ah, the very thing I've been wanting to mention."

"You have?" Drat, how did she make such a mull of this? The one thing she wanted to avoid was a declaration from Mac. Once she would have been tempted to accept; once she would have wept for the offer. He was still the same charming companion—at least before tonight—with the same ready smile and devil-may-care attitude. It was her attitude that had changed, no, her perspective, finally ready to look beneath the surface, past the laughing, empty eyes. That new cynicism told her that it was only a matter of time before Mac realized he could avoid paying rent altogether if he married the landlady. Obviously he'd found the time.

"Mac, please don't say anything more. Marriage is too . . . too important a step."

"Marriage? Who said anything about marriage?" He scratched his head, trying to remember. His fingers found a lock of hair and twirled it round and round.

"Oh, then you don't wish to marry me?" Cristabel was too relieved to feel humiliated for her misinterpretation.

"Well, I'd like to, of course. I mean you're a devilish good-looking woman now and all, and comfortable besides, not always making scenes and nattering on at a fellow. You're a real lady, Belle, and a chap could do a lot worse, if he was looking to get leg-shackled."

"Thank you, Major. That's very kind, even if I did back you into the corner."

"Not at all. The thing is, I cannot really afford a wife, a poor wife, that is. I don't suppose you have a handsome dowry tucked away somewhere? Old Harwood didn't make a deposit for you before he stuck his spoon in the wall or anything?"

Cristabel had to laugh. Here was cream-pot love, indeed! "I only wish he did, Mac, but I'm as poor as a church-mouse myself, or as near as makes no difference. I have to start advertising for music pupils soon."

"But what if there was another way? See, it's like Kitty and Gwen and all the girls with no dowries, no families to take them in, and no connections. They've got no chance of making a respectable match so they have to earn their own keep, same as you or I. Now, there are men, well-heeled men with more money than Golden Ball, who are willing, no, happy, to spend their blunt for some pretty companionship."

"Mac, what are you saying? Those men, the officers, Kitty's Lord Minerly, they *pay* the girls?"

"No, no, that would be vulgar. A woman needs a man to handle these things for her."

"Mac, the girls? Tell me, please, that I don't understand what you're saying, that they're not, not light-skirts."

"They don't walk the streets, if that's what you're

thinking. Nick and I make sure no one gets out of line and—"

"Nick and you? *My house?*"

"I know you're upset right now, Belle, but think about it. With a careful adviser and the right introductions, a good-looking woman can do very well for herself."

Miss Swann stood. Curtsied like a duchess. And tipped the punch bowl into Major MacDermott's lap.

"Dash it, Kenley, you've been looking like thunder all night. If you're not going to enjoy yourself, why did we come to Vauxhall? We could have gone to Lady Ingleston's rout and not enjoyed ourselves."

"I told you, Perry, I'm just not ready to face all the toadeaters of the *ton*. If it's not the young pups wanting to hear war stories, it's the hopeful mamas pushing their simpering misses at me."

"Well, you are a hero, and the biggest prize to come on the marriage market for years. You can't blame 'em."

"But I don't have to like them, either. I'm just not ready for the polite world, Almack's and all its rules, the insipid debutantes and the inadequate refreshments. Besides, I really wanted to see the fireworks, and the thousand lanterns that are supposed to be here."

"And one particular bit of fluff?"

Winstoke smiled ruefully. "Who isn't insipid and who seems to make her own rules. She dances like an angel, too."

"Yes, so you've had your dance. It didn't make you any better company, so can we go? Look, your angel is leaving anyway."

"Blast, the little fool is going off by herself again."

"So? She's most likely just looking for the convenience."

"Down the Dark Walk? I am going to keelhaul that nodcock MacDermott."

"Come on, Kenley, you can't worry about a jade like that. She knows what she's doing."

"And I'd swear she doesn't."

Oh dear, where was the exit? She had thought it was this way when she rushed off, but she couldn't see the pavilion or the fortune-teller's tent, and there were less lights than she remembered. She could hear the music though, so if she just took this side-path back, she should do fine. Except for the two men blocking her way.

"Hey, mate, what have we here?"

"It looks like our lucky night, don't it?"

Cristabel took one horrified look at the blackened teeth, the torn gloves and rag-stuffed shoes, the leering, unshaven faces—and turned to race back the way she had come. As fast as she could run, the thugs were gaining. She was gasping for every breath—and they were laughing! One was close enough to grab at her dress. She could hear the gauze overskirt rip, and still she ran—straight into Lord Winstoke's arms!

"My, my," he said, holding her close for just a moment before setting her behind him, "you do have a full dance card tonight, don't you?"

"Hey, mister, we seen her first."

"And I bet I've seen the Indian Ocean before you. That doesn't make it mine, either."

"Please, my lord, oh please can we not just go?" Cristabel said, tugging on his sleeve, trembling.

He touched her bare arm reassuringly, but told her, "I'm afraid it won't be that simple, will it, gentlemen?"

"Not unless you wants to make it up to us with some of the ready."

"I'll pay! Whatever you want. Here." Cristabel fumbled with the strings of her reticule.

"Poor Bluebell, don't you remember your nursery stories? The ones where the trolls hid under the bridge and travelers had to pay to cross? The travelers always got made into porridge anyway, you know. No, there's only one way to deal with the ogres of the world." He removed his jacket and handed it to her. "Just one favor, lads, try not to hit my head if you can."

The first brute rushed straight for the viscount, swinging for his skull. Winstoke ducked beneath the blow and brought his own fist up, straight to the fellow's jaw. When that one hit the ground, the other ruffian came on with a cudgel, raised high. Before he could bring it down, Winstoke's fist was buried in his stomach, knocking all the air out of him. Cristabel was still looking for a stick, a rock, anything to throw, to protect her champion, when he laughed and took his jacket out of her clenched hands.

"I suggest we leave now, unless you want to wait for your friends to wake up."

"Of all the cork-brained, caper-witted things to do! You may as well have told them you were wounded!"

"Right, maybe next time."

"You . . . you great looby. It's not that I don't appreciate what you did. I don't know what would have happened if you hadn't . . . but they could have hurt you!"

That concern in her voice was worth the skinned knuckles, but Winstoke only smiled. "Tactics, my girl," he told her. "If you tell a bully about a weakness, he'll go right for it, making it that much easier to protect. You know just where he's aiming. If you're going to cut up stiff at me, though, your coming down here alone wasn't exactly needle-witted, especially after you saw what could happen right on the dance floor. Whatever possessed you to run off by yourself like that?"

Little things: her house was a bordello, her friends were light-skirts and panderers, and the only offer she was ever likely to get was *carte blanche*. It was too overwhelming and mortifying to discuss. "Just say that I am as ignorant as a turnip and I've made mice feet out of everything."

"As bad as all that, hm?"

"Worse!"

"I know it's trite, but things often do look better after a good night's sleep. Anyone would be overset after such a frightening experience."

Miss Swann didn't know how she was ever to sleep in that house again, but she couldn't tell the viscount that. "Do you think I could trouble you to find me a hackney? I doubt Major MacDermott waited for me."

"I have my carriage," he offered, consigning Perry to a hired coach.

"You've already been so kind, my lord, I—"

"Do you think you might call me something other than 'my lord'? Winstoke would be fine, even Lee. That's what my mother calls me."

"Thank you, Lee, but—"

"Yes, you've already thanked me, and no, it's not out of my way. And if it will set your mind at rest, your virtue is safe with me." He added a mental "Tonight," but quickly appended, "While I am being so avuncular, a bit of advice: just like these ruffians back there, men cannot resist a challenge. Your air of innocence in a siren's body is just that. Your cloak of gentility is a dare."

"But I *am* respectable." At least she thought so, before tonight.

If he privately thought she had last been innocent in

the cradle maybe, he only agreed with her: "Whatever
you say, sweetheart."

"You don't believe me, do you?"

"I don't know what I believe anymore, to be honest,
but it doesn't matter. I do know that I am well and truly
caught in your spell."

"Here, put this around you. You're trembling."

Cristabel had left her wrap back at the box, for all the
warmth another piece of netting would have been. She
huddled into the carriage blanket he draped over her
shoulders, even knowing her shivers weren't from the
night chill alone.

"Don't think about those men," the viscount told her,
putting his arm around her to keep the blanket secure.

What men? Lord Minerly, Sir Winklesham, Mr. Frye?
How could she not think about them, coming in and out
of her house? And what Mac wanted her to do—she
shuddered again.

"Here," Winstoke soothed, pulling her closer into the
security of his arms. "You are safe now."

Heaven knew what she would have to face in Kensington, or how she would prove to this nobleman that
things weren't what they seemed, but for this moment she
did feel safe and reassured. She relaxed against him with
a sigh.

By Jupiter, Winstoke asked himself, feeling her soft-
ness against his chest, inhaling her lavender scent, did I
really swear to honor her virtue?

The ride was too long for Winstoke, too short for Miss
Swann. It was too long for him to hold this most desirable
woman in his arms without seeing if the skin above that

absurd butterfly was as soft as it looked, or without feeling those velvet lips respond to his again.

And the ride was too short to face the unpleasantness outside of his strong embrace, to leave the security and the tingle in her stomach at his nearness. Cristabel barely had time to wonder if he would kiss her, if she turned her face up to his, and if she would stop him.

Then they were in Kensington, and the driver was asking for the address. Cristabel directed him for several blocks, and then told him to halt at the corner of Sullivan Street. She could see the house up ahead—anyone could, it was so well lighted, with several carriages out front. There was no way she wanted Lord Winstoke to witness the scene she was sure would follow, and maybe he didn't even know about the house yet. It was such a long shot Uncle Charlie would turn over in his grave, but it was her only hope.

"Here will be fine," she told him, tumbling out of the carriage as soon as the footman had the door open, before the viscount could get down to assist her. "I wouldn't want to wake anyone, you see. And you've done so much and thank you, and please excuse me." And she hurried off into the darkness.

Bemused, the viscount ordered his coachman to follow, slowly and at a distance. Cristabel was too fired up to notice, by the time she pushed past two soldiers watering the flower bed. No wonder nothing grew here!

Chapter Eleven

Locked! Her own front door was locked against her! Cristabel rapped, but they were playing the pianoforte and singing too loudly inside to hear. So she pounded on the door with both fists and yelled, "Nick Blass, you open the door this instant, you miserable whoremonger!"

They heard that, all right. In the parlor and across the street, where Lord Winstoke sat in his carriage, chuckling.

"Shall we drive on now, milord?" his coachman asked, offended. This was no place for the quality.

"No, let's wait. I might get to see fireworks tonight after all." He laughed. Damn, the chit had spirit. For an instant he was reminded of Harwood's dragon niece, breathing hellfire and moral outrage. Lord, he hoped she was behind one of the lace curtains he saw being twitched aside, up and down the street. He'd pay another share of Harwood's debts just to see her face, if she heard his little spitfire and found she was living next door to a brothel! He'd have to remember to ask Jonas Sparling in the morning for the old harridan's address. Meanwhile, the front door of Belle's house was opening, and he strained to hear the conversation.

* * *

"Out. I want them out, do you hear me? All of them! You have ten minutes to get rid of them, and another five to gather your things. Then I'll call the watch and the constable and every magistrate in the city."

"So Sleepin' Beauty finally 'as 'er eyes open. Well, it's too late, missy, too late 'n too bad. You're one of us now. Mac was right for once: there's not a bloody thing you can do about it."

"I'll never be one of you! I'd burn this house down before I'd see it used like this."

"Fancy words from a fancy piece don't make you no better'n you should be neither. It was your uncle as put this place in business. We had an agreement. 'E got to visit the girls for free, 'stead of collectin' rent."

"I'll make you a new agreement, you despicable little worm: you get out of here now and I won't bring charges against you for what you've stolen from me in rents and coal money and heaven knows what else. Otherwise I'll see you deported, you and your foul-stenched cigars and all."

Nick raised his shaggy brows to look behind her out the still open door, through which a crowd of people was rushing, some of the men straightening clothes, some of the girls dragging hurriedly packed trunks, lace edges hanging out. Nick's crafty eyes noted the crest on the big carriage out there across the street, and knew he was outmanned, for now.

"You brung the 'eavy artillery to back you up, so I'll go, wench, but you shut the barn door too late. You think your deuced 'ero's gonna come up to scratch, you got 'ay in your cockloft. No swell's takin' 'is mistress to wife, 'n 'e sure as 'ell ain't takin' anyone else's mistress. I'll tell the world'n its grandma how you been hangin' on Mac's sleeve. And I'll tell you somethin' else, missy. You ain't

seen the last of Nick Blass, you ain't. I don't care about
your deeds and your lawyers, you ain't gonna live in my
house. Not long, you ain't."

Shaking, Cristabel looked around. The parlor was
empty, and the hall contained only a pale-faced Fanny
and Boy, peering around the back of the stairway. Not
much in the way of reinforcements.

"Boy, do you want to be porter and odd-job man?" she
called out. He nodded. "Then you follow this gallows-
bait and make sure he doesn't take anything that doesn't
belong to him. And you, Fanny, if you want to stay here
at all, you go wash that paint off your face and you guard
the door. I don't want any more of these mongrels in here
again, is that clear?"

"Oh yes, Miss Cristabel."

"Good. I'll have a few more words to speak to you
later, you can be sure of that," Cristabel told the girl,
making her face go whiter still, enough so her freckles
stood out, even under the rouge.

The troops deployed if not rallied, Cristabel made for
the stairway. She doubted anyone could have slept
through the party, much less her latest skirmish, but she
was determined to make a clean sweep, no quarter given.

"You lied to me. I thought you were my friend and you
lied to me. You stood right by and let me ruin myself.
How could you do that?"

Marie was packing. It was taking her longer than the
other girls because of all her sewing supplies; she was
trying to stuff too many odd bits of fabric into too few
hat boxes and satchels. Feathers kept escaping, and buttons were all over the floor. So was Marie, in a heap,
sobbing.

"I didn't want to, I swear I didn't want to."

"Then why? You were so good to me about my hair and everything, and when I was sickly. I thought you cared. Was it just the money?"

"Oh no, never that! I would have done all I could anyway, you were so sweet and kindhearted." Marie started to weep again.

"Oh stop that, do. Here." Cristabel offered her own handkerchief, miraculously still dry. "Now tell me."

Marie sniffled. "It was funny, at first. I mean, you were so proper, it was like a joke having you here, and we all thought you'd leave right away when you got better, with no harm done, but you didn't. And then it was too late. Nick . . ."

"What about Nick? You can tell me, he's gone, for good if he knows what's healthy for him."

"Nick made us swear not to tell you, all of us. Some of the girls didn't care; they didn't know about a lady's reputation and all. They never had any. I said it was wrong, I really did."

"I believe you, but then why did you go along with them?"

"I had no choice," Marie wailed, burying her face in the handkerchief again. "Nick scared me. He said he'd hire me out for a barracks party, if I told. I couldn't have stood it, Miss Cristabel, I just couldn't."

Now Cristabel was really near tears herself. "But Marie, he couldn't have forced you to."

"You don't understand. I have no money, no place else in the world I can go. If it weren't for this house, I'd have to be standing on the corner outside Drury Lane with the other doxies."

"Marie, no. You're not a, a . . ."

"Yes, I am! I never wanted to be, but I am. At least here I only have to go with men I want."

"I thought your mother was in service to a noble house. Couldn't you have gotten a position, instead?"

"Why do you think I left my family?" Marie asked bitterly. "Because I was growing up! His noble lordship took to noticing me, if you know what I mean. My mother would have been dismissed if she'd complained. She was lucky enough to have a job that let her keep a child at all. So she found me a place as abigail with a family in London. A family with sons. I couldn't stay, but I couldn't go home. So I decided I was already ruined, let the dastards pay for it, instead of taking it for free. I had a chance for something better, though."

"Your beau?"

Marie just nodded miserably. "Lord Radway."

"A nobleman? I mean, did he really say he would marry you?"

"Oh no, I never—that is, he's already married."

"Forgive me, I should have known," Cristabel said, but Marie missed the sarcasm.

"We talked about a little place of my own. I thought I could put some money aside, if I didn't have to pay rent, and do dressmaking for extra."

"To save for your pension?"

"Exactly. But he's not back yet from the country, and I don't know where to go, and I'm so sorry I had to lie to you."

"Stop being such a watering pot! I understand how Nick frightened you, he scared me half to death, downstairs. Really I do. And . . . and I cannot like your plans, but you may stay here until your Lord Radway comes for you."

"Oh thank you, and you don't need to worry, I'll be as proper as a parson till Chauncey comes."

"Chauncey?"

Marie just shrugged. "You know, this was an awful thing to do to you, and all, and I would have sent you off if I could, but then I kept hoping something good might come of it. Your Lord Winstoke is so handsome and rich—"

"So what is there not to love, right? If you think that's the perfect answer, that I'd accept a slip on the shoulder in order to secure my future, you better keep packing. That's not love. That's no future either, Marie, and I *do* have a choice."

Fanny was in the parlor downstairs, holding Major MacDermott at bay with the fireplace poker.

"You told me to keep the mongrels out, miss, but you didn't say if it was just strays."

"You did fine. Did Nick leave?"

"Yes, ma'am, cursing something terrible, he was. Boy locked all the doors and windows, though, and set his watchdog loose downstairs."

"Boy has a watchdog?"

"Oh yes, a great ferocious beast it is, too. Do you want to see?"

"Uh, not right now. I'd like to talk to the major first."

Mac was not looking like his usual well turned-out self. His hair stood in disheveled peaks, the front of his jacket, waistcoat, and pantaloons had a big red splotch, and his laced neckcloth that had been tied in a Waterfall looked more like a whirlpool. He was nervously twisting a piece of net fabric between his hands, her scarf.

"I looked for you everywhere. You shouldn't have gone off like that."

Fanny's eyes were wide with curiosity, so Cristabel sent her to fetch some tea.

"No," Cristabel decided, "I think I need something stronger. I am quite sure there is something drinkable right here, in my own parlor." This last was spoken with such venom you'd think Napoleon had just landed his invasion force there. "Could you please just bring me a clean glass, Fanny? Make that two," she said, looking at Mac again, then told the maid to wait. "I'd like to hear your story first."

"My story, ma'am?"

"Yes, you know, how you happened to be here, why you went along with all the lies instead of telling me the truth about this place, when I was the one paying your salary."

Fanny looked at Mac, who looked away. Then she kept her eyes on her feet. "I didn't like to lie, Miss Cristabel. On my honor. I don't suppose that's saying much, anymore. On my mother's honor, I didn't like misleading you. Nick said I had to or he'd sell me to one of the flash houses."

"What? You can't sell little girls, not even in this wicked city!" She turned to Mac for confirmation, but he was only looking grayer in the face and wouldn't meet her eyes either.

"You see how easy it was to keep it from you, Miss Cristabel? You're greener than I was even. I thought I could find honest work here, a strong farm girl and all, 'cause there were too many of us at home and not enough to go around. My Uncle Samuel, he's the one with the wooden leg, was bringing some cane work up to town to sell, so I rode along with him. Nick was at the market and asked did I want a job. I didn't know any better, and when I did, I was only glad he wasn't one of the ones what drug girls and keep them locked up. I never wanted to be there, ma'am, even if it meant fibbing."

"I understand, child. Go fetch the glasses."

If she were judge and jury, by the look Cristabel gave Mac, he was hanged.

"But, Belle," he protested in his own defense, "Nick wanted to kill you and I wouldn't let him."

"I suppose I have that much to be thankful for, then, Major MacDermott. And it is Miss Swann to you."

"Ah, come on, Belle, you're carrying on like I stole the crown jewels. It's not that bad, my dear."

"No? Mac, I have no money except a temporary loan. I have no family and no connections. I had two things left, this house and my good name, and that's what you stole. I think that's bad enough."

"But I can make it up to you, Belle. We'll get married! That would fix it all right and tight. It's what I always wanted, you know, so you'd be making me the happiest of men."

"Cut line, Mac, it's too late to turn me up sweet. I'd sooner take the kitchen cat to bed or marry Attila the Hun. But tell me something, before you start packing. What hold did Nick Blass have over you? I mean, you were an officer, with a good education, a respectable family, a sure future. Why would you do such a thing?" She waved her hand around to mean the house, the girls, not just herself.

"The money, of course, always the money. It's like this: I hate the Army. The British despise the Scots still, so my regiment is always sent into the thick of things. I don't want to go back there to be cannon fodder. But if I sell out, Uncle cuts off my income."

"So this is by way of being a new career? Instead of

the Army, instead of finding an honest position some-where, you tried to make your fortune off the women?"

"No, no. I tried to explain to you before. It's the men who pay. The girls were going to be, ah, in business any-way. I just found them a better class of customers, you might say."

"You make me sick. Get your things and get out."

"Now hold, Belle. You cannot just toss me out. I had a lease with Lord Harwood, and I'm paid for this quarter."

"Show me the contract."

"Devil a bit, it was a gentlemen's agreement. We shook hands."

"Since neither one of you was much of a gentleman, I'd say the lease is void. This is my house, and it will be respectable. You're not. You'll have to go."

"But Belle—Miss Swann," he corrected, seeing the harsh frown, "it's only for a week or so more before I'll have to rejoin my unit. I can't claim sick leave much longer."

"No."

"But you need me here," he said, thinking quickly. "I can keep all the regulars away and pass the word that the girls are all gone."

"You can do that from the barracks."

"What about Nick, then? Do you think he was bam-ming, with all those threats? Let me tell you, he doesn't have a whole lot of respect for the value of human lives, if you get my drift. And he was madder than I've ever seen him. Or did you expect to protect yourself with those two children"—he gestured out the hall—"Fanny with a poker and Boy with a skillet?"

"I'll notify the watch, then, or go to Bow Street."

"What's the watch going to do, circle the block an extra time? And how long will your money last if you have to hire runners to guard the house twenty-four hours a day? 'Cause Nick'll be back, you can bet on it."

Cristabel couldn't agree, not with her threats of legal action against him, yet the filthy skirter might be demented enough to try to intimidate her again. The thought of that foul little man coming anywhere near her was enough to turn her stomach to knots. Mac saw his advantage.

"Think on it, *ma belle,* I have a pistol and a sword. I'll protect you with my life. It's the least I can do if you won't let me do the honorable by giving you my name."

His name was as sullied as hers, but he did have a point, a sharp one that with any luck he knew how to use.

"Very well, Major," she decided, "you may stay until you rejoin your regiment. I hope to rent your suite, of course, so you will have to move to the top floor."

"But Belle, my leg!"

"Gammon, Major. I have seen you dance. It's the top floor or nothing. That's a lot more in keeping with the rent you've paid anyway, if you ever did. And it's Miss Swann."

"You're a hard woman, my—Miss Swann."

"One more thing, Major MacDermott. You will also make it a point to inform Lord Winstoke that we were never, ah, intimate. Your friend Nick intends to spread that lie in his direction."

"Nick's got no need to. Winstoke's no greenhorn, he'll assume it's true anyway."

"All the more reason for you to tell him otherwise!"

"Wind blows in that quarter, huh? You'd do a lot better to have me, if you're waiting to bring that downy bird up to scratch. He could have done the right thing by you ages ago, if he chose. Matter of fact, he got you into this mess, not me or Nick."

"I don't know what you're talking about."

"It's the way of the world, Belle. Face it, he can look a lot higher, and he will."

It's the way of the world. How many times had Cristabel heard that? And always in conjunction with something terrible, like the good die young, and poverty only breeds poverty. It wasn't fair! And that, too, was the way of the world. Pounding on her pillow wasn't going to change a thing, only make her even more exhausted after this long, sleepless night.

What a fool she'd been. What a blind, buffleheaded, harebrained fool! There were all those questions she should have been asking, all those answers she hadn't wanted to hear. Being stupid was even worse than being ruined. Maybe. She'd had a great deal of help in losing her reputation: people did lie to her and miscolor the truth. She had no one else to blame for being witless, however, only herself.

She'd been too busy being frivolous, that's what. She had let herself be carried along by the fun and excitement, like a little girl in her mother's dresses, playing at grown-up games. Too many schoolgirl dreams after all, she supposed, or too many of those purple-covered romances. Whatever, she'd forgotten to keep her feet solidly on the ground, she'd forgotten the way of the world. Now everything was ruined, most of all her dreams.

Winstoke could look higher, Mac had said. Of course he could. Gently bred females didn't come much lower, but he had looked, for all that. He had sought her company, and as a lady, not as a *chérie amour.* She was sure of it. Hadn't he protected her honor and kept her safe? Hadn't he held her so she felt . . . She didn't want to think about how she felt in his arms, not if she would never feel them again! But if Mac was right, the viscount knew all about the house. If he knew about the girls, he would have to think she was one of them, even without Nick's poisonous lies. And if he thought that . . . There was no hope. That was the way of the world.

Chapter Twelve

It was a new chapter. It had to be, if Cristabel was to have any life at all. She hadn't left Miss Meadow's drudgery to wallow in gloom and self-pity in London, had she? No, she had not, she firmly announced to herself the next morning, putting her feet on the floor and wincing at the sore head that announced itself back.

No matter. She would get on with making her surroundings look respectable, which she should have done ages ago before being seduced from her purpose by worldly gaiety and smooth-tongued temptations. She had *not* been seduced; that was the important thing. She may have been compromised—No, she amended honestly, she may have compromised herself past redemption, but only with the high echelons of the *ton*, which she had no hopes of entering anyway, with neither sponsor nor dowry. She was already beyond the pale, being in trade. At least she would see it was an honest trade!

Even before dressing, she sat down at her desk and wrote the following: "Furnished rooms and suites available at reasonable rates to persons of refinement. Also, music instruction on pianoforte and harp for young ladies. Inquire: 15 Sullivan Street, Kensington."

Then she went out to the hallway and called for Fanny.

Not knowing what to expect after last night, Fanny cautiously edged down the stairs.

"Good morning, Fanny. Is Major MacDermott awake yet?"

"What, him? I expect he'll lie abed till noon, like usual."

"The devil he will. You'll please see that he is up and stirring, Fanny. Tell him that I need him to deliver this to the newspaper office while he is at that other errand we spoke about last night. He'll know the one."

"You mean going to tell that there viscount how you and Mac—"

"Fanny, you weren't listening, were you?"

"Didn't have to, ma'am. Mac kept going on about it while we carried his stuff upstairs. He didn't think it was such a good idea."

"That's the best recommendation I've heard yet. Go on, and when you get back we are going to start house-cleaning, before anyone answers the advertisement. This place is a disgrace." She opened the front door to show Fanny what she meant. "There are the windows, and the front walk, and the railings, to start. Why, respectable people wouldn't even look inside."

"Pardon me, Miss Cristabel, but if you're hoping to improve what folks think, maybe you should consider putting your slippers on at least, afore you go inspecting the outside in your nightclothes."

"Saucy minx," Cristabel laughed, quickly closing the door and running back to her rooms to change. Mops and brooms would have to wait while she looked through her heavy old schoolmistress dresses in the back of the closet. No matter what, she would never give up her pretty new gowns, even if she did ask Marie to fill in the necklines somewhat. There was no rule saying a landlady couldn't be fashionable. She would never wear that heavy black serge gown again, no, not even to be buried in! She pulled it out of the closet, thinking to use it for rags, when she had a better idea, except in Fanny's opinion.

"What? You mean I'm to wear that musty old thing and stick to you like a leech?"

"No, I mean Marie is going to make a proper maid's uniform out of it and you will wear it when you accompany me in the park and when you answer the door and curtsy to all the people who will answer the ad."

"But it's so plain and ugly, no one will notice me," wailed the poor girl.

"No one is supposed to notice the maid, you gudgeon," Marie told her. "She is just there for appearance sake."

Fanny hefted the gown before lifting it over her head so Marie could pin it. "There's so much of it I don't know how I'll even walk. Why I bet it'll be like what happened to my mother's Aunt Margaret. She saved half her days for a wedding gown, but her husband-to-be's mother died in childhood, like they say in the country. So when she turned forty she had the village seamstress make her up the fanciest black dress you ever did see, enough fabric for two, maybe three gowns, to wear to church on special Sundays."

"And what happened?" Cristabel asked, knowing Fanny's tales never ended so easily.

"First day she wore it, she took the long way home, to make sure all the neighbors got a good look, you know. She got tired, though, adragging all that material around with her, so she took a shortcut back, on the stepping stones over the creek. Only her feet got caught up in the hem and in she went. Dress sopped up water like a sponge and weighed her right down. Drowned she did, in three feet of water. They had to wait three days for the dress to dry, too, 'fore they could bury her in it."

When she was done laughing, Cristabel promised she hadn't meant Fanny to look like a hired mourner, and Marie agreed to try for a modish look. There was so much extra fabric, Fanny being a little dab of a thing, according to Marie, that there would be enough for one dress and another skirt, especially if she filled the skirt's hem with some white lace ruffle she happened to have. She knew just where they could purchase a tiny pink apron and lace cap to go with the dress uniform, and those pink ribbons left over from Cristabel's carriage dress . . . Fanny was all smiles again. It was time to get to work.

Boy was set to scrubbing the steps after being measured for a new shirt, which would come after a bath, after the house was clean. He may as well get used to soap and water, Cristabel informed him, vowing to throw as many of his pets as she could catch into the tub with him.

Cristabel had inked out two neat new signs to be placed in the front windows as soon as Fanny was through washing them, inside and out, and Marie had already soaked the parlor curtains and was laying them on that small patch of lawn in front to bleach in the sun before she would start the sewing.

And Miss Swann was polishing the brass. She was wearing her ugliest old gown, the brown bombazine with stains on it, and a huge apron found in the kitchen, no less spotted, and part of her old ragged shawl wrapped around her head like a scarf to keep her hair from getting in the cleaning solution. The scarf kept falling into her eyes, though, so she kept pushing it up with wet, grimy hands, leaving streaks up and down her face. But didn't that door knocker gleam!

She was starting on the railings when one of the neighbor's doors opened and a woman holding a little boy by the hand came out. A nursery maid followed, pushing a pram. They were obviously on the way to the park—the boy had a wooden ball—and had to pass Cristabel's house. They did, but crossed to the other side of the street first, the mother giving the boy's arm a good jerk to keep him from even looking at the house.

There were a few more wet streaks down Cristabel's cheeks, but she found that one didn't actually die of shame, no more than of a broken heart. It was a good thing that railing was brass clean through; she'd have scoured off any plating long since.

One set of windows was sparkling, so Miss Swann took time to prop the new ROOMS sign there, only smearing one corner with damp hands. Determinedly, she marched back to the railing, starting Fanny and Boy's lessons at the same time.

"Do you see that first letter? That is an *R*. *R* as in *rooms*. Say it after me. *R* as in *rooms*. *R* as in *respectable*."

By the time they were all giggling again over *M* as in *Miss* Fanny, *M* as in *Mister* Boy, Cristabel had her first lodger. With an *L,* as in *legitimate*.

"But the ad was only sent in this morning," she told the thin, bespectacled young man standing in front of her. He seemed to be about nineteen, and nervous. "You couldn't have seen it yet."

"Except that I work at the paper, miss! It's my lunch break, and I hurried over. I don't know that Mr. Helfhopher would approve. He's the editor, you know."

Cristabel liked the young man on sight. He was neatly groomed, in a serviceable brown jacket and an unassuming, if inexpertly tied, cravat. She'd been fooled by appearance before, though, so she asked Mr. Haynes so many questions he finally had to beg her to take his deposit on the smallest, cheapest top-floor room before he was late getting back to work and lost his job altogether.

Mr. Haynes was a journalist, aspiring. There were so many stories he wanted to write, ones he knew Mr. Helfhopher would buy, if only he had a quiet place to compose.

This was the place, and Mr. Haynes and Miss Swann shook hands on the deal, adding printer's ink to Cristabel's accumulated filth.

It was the *S* that was Cristabel's downfall. That slippery, sneaky *S* just didn't have a proper sound to it. She was so tired by then with the unaccustomed hard physical work, that she just couldn't think past *silk, seducer, sin.* She sank down onto the marble steps next to Boy's bucket to finish the bottom half of the very last rail. Put the pasty stuff on, wipe it off. Up and down, up and down. Up was all shiny, down was . . . a pair of black leather boots.

"Excuse me, I'd like to see one of the women who lives here."

Without even looking up, Cristabel angrily responded, "They are all gone. None of them are here anymore, so you can go on about your business."

To which Lord Winstoke, not used to such rudeness from servants, demanded, "The mistress of the house then."

"There are certainly no mistresses, and never will be!" She pushed the scarf back so she could look up. "And if

you don't go away I'll—Lord Winstoke, good morning.
You came."

There was that smile, the crooked one that said I know
you're not a noddy, just adorably confused, the one that
said of course I came. The words, however, said, "Or
you'll what?"

She could only stand and grin, especially when he
pulled a snowy handkerchief from his pocket and wiped
at the smudges on her face.

"Or I'll get you dirty." .

"My, my, I think I can risk it." He looked around and
saw a lanky, dark-skinned youth staring wide-eyed at
him, and the saucy little freckle-puss maid he recognized
from walks in the park, all swaddled in rags, winking
from over by the windows. Even that woman Marie was
there, on the other side of the window, rubbing the glass
with old newspapers, smiling, and nodding. "Could we
go inside and talk?"

Cristabel saw her crew relaxing and frowned them
back to work. She also saw safety in their numbers. Inside, alone . . . she remembered the feel of his arms
around her. "No. I mean no, thank you, I have to finish
this."

"It's fairly private, what I have to say."

"I cannot imagine anything that cannot properly be
said in front of my friends."

The "properly" should have tipped Winstoke off, but
he assumed they'd heard proposals such as his many
times before. He hadn't made one, ever, and was not
quite sure how to proceed, except in a whisper, with the
whole motley bunch pretending not to listen.

"Miss Belle, you have to know how, ah, deeply I regard you."

Cristabel twisted the rag in her hands. Why did she have to be dressed like a washerwoman?

"And I think that you return my regard?"

She nodded shyly, holding her breath. Drat, she should have taken him inside after all.

"I hoped so. I couldn't help noticing that you were in some difficulties last evening and it pained me to see you distressed." The viscount reached his limit with the stilted control of being overheard. Zounds, he'd been agonizing over the emotional decision for hours—no, days, ever since he'd first seen this maddeningly beautiful, beguiling woman. "Belle, dearest," he breathed, forgetting the audience entirely, "let me take care of you, and cherish you, and show you all the joy two people can share."

Cristabel's heart was singing. She closed her eyes to see her dream come true. "Forever and ever."

"Forever?"

Her eyes snapped open. "Forever. How long did you think marriage lasted?"

Now he remembered the listeners and blushed for the first time he could remember. "Belle," he said, barely audibly, "even you know better than that."

"Even I? Even I, the last person to know anything around here? Well, Mr. High and Mighty, despite what others said, even I didn't think you were low enough to make me an *indecent* proposal." She was shouting, she was so angry. That little boy in the park must have heard; the cleaners stopped pretending and just sat listening.

"Come now, Belle," he reasoned, trying to reclaim her usual serene nature. "You know I could not propose marriage. I owe my family and my name more than that."

Those blue eyes glimmered in fury, at him and at herself, for foolishly hoping again the moment she saw that loving smile. It was loving, too, she just knew it. Only it was the wrong kind of love, the brass-plated kind that would wear off. The cheap, pinchbeck version, that's what this miserable swine was offering her. "And what about my honor? What if I had a noble, proud old name, even if you never bothered to ask it!"

Winstoke's flaming ears picked up the first part, and that rankled. "What honor, living here under MacDermott's protection?"

"I live under no man's protection, my lord!"

He was as angry as she now, thinking of her with that court-card. "And you don't live in his house?"

"This is *my* house, and I *am* a respectable woman, and let me tell you this, I am blessed tired of telling that to people! I don't know why everyone wants to assume the worst about me, and I may have been ignorant, but I *do* come from a good family and I have *never* done anything that would make them ashamed of me, like offering *carte blanche* to a gently reared female, my lord." Cristabel took a deep breath and continued:

"Furthermore, I would never, no matter how dire my circumstances, accept cupboard kisses from a man who would hide me away in a little love nest somewhere while he danced at all the grand balls with 'eligible' females and even married one. If that is a sign of your 'deep regard,' my lord, then your heart is as black as your moral character. You, sir, are a rake and a libertine. I pray I never see you again. Good day."

With that, she kicked over Boy's bucket, stormed inside, slammed down the other front window, and slapped her second sign into place.

It wasn't the sign that did the trick. Lord Winstoke's jaw had been hanging open long before he read "Music instruction, pianoforte and harp."

It wasn't even the references to a noble, proud name

that finally registered with his addled mind, a name that he had never asked and supposedly didn't know.

It wasn't the moral lesson, either, although that clinched it.

What turned the tide was that one piercing statement, "It's *my* house." His heart in his mouth, which he finally closed, Lord Winstoke was certain he knew Belle's name after all, and all too well.

•

Chapter Thirteen

His new boots were ruined and his feet were sopping wet and cold inside them. Lord Winstoke's temper, however, was on the boil.

"Jonas Sparling," he commanded at the top of his considerable lungs, squelching across the marble hallway. "Report to the bridge."

If nothing else, the order cleared the decks of every other of his lordship's servants, especially quickly those used to gentry who delicately tugged the bellpull when they wished service.

Sparling skidded to a halt on the now-puddled marble. "Aye-aye, Cap'n. Uh, you called, my lord?" Sparling was more curious than perturbed. He had seen the captain in combat before, unlike the rest of the lubbers on board. As cool as the breeze off Dover, Captain Chase was during a battle, so at least they were not under attack by French warships right in Mayfair, as a body might suppose from all the hurly-burly below stairs. This was something personal, and, hell, whatever had the captain's nose out of joint, he could only fire a valet, he couldn't make him walk the plank. So Jonas nodded toward his master's boots and asked if he should batten the hatches, with a rough sea following.

"I'll batten your hatches, you yardarm yahoo. By all

that's holy, man, why didn't you tell me Miss Swann was a young lady? A beautiful, charming, refined lady?"

"You wouldn't listen, Cap'n."

"Gads, Jonas, I was blind, not deaf!"

"You ordered me not to mention her name to you, sir."

"Sailor, do you know how Lord Nelson won his promotion?"

"Yes, sir, I expect every man in the Navy knows about the Battle of the Baltic."

Winstoke ignored him. "I'll tell you. He disobeyed orders, that's how. He held his telescope up to his missing eye and said he couldn't see Admiral Parker's signal to withdraw. He stayed to fight, for the good of his country. He went on to win the battle, got made a viscount and commander of the whole Channel fleet . . . by disobeying orders."

"You made me promise, my lord."

"But a bordello, man! You had to have known I'd sent an innocent maiden off to live in a brothel!"

"You begged."

"Floyd, another bottle." The viscount was in his study, slouched in a soft chair, his bare feet toasting by the fire. He'd already finished one bottle, but he was still thinking clearly. Too clearly, for sobriety only told him that he was now the two men Miss Swann liked least in all of England. One had stolen her inheritance, the other kept trying for her virtue. Lord, let there be oblivion in the brandy.

He would have had her anyway, he realized now, too late, even if she weren't pure. Now he couldn't have her any way, neither mistress nor wife. She would only believe his proposal came from a sense of honor, if she heard him out at all, to give her his name. Worse, she'd believe he was only offering marriage to get what was unobtainable otherwise. She would never believe he couldn't live without her.

It was true, though, astonishing as it was. Love had come to the captain, and he had no defense. He had tried valiantly, of course, calling it lust, infatuation, then the pleasure of the chase. He was playing her game, he had told himself, while she held out for higher stakes. But there was no game, and the only stake Miss Swann understood was a wedding band. He should have known. Her kiss was that of an innocent, he could swear for him alone. Fool that he was, he had let his pride deal himself out. Where were his pride and his family honor now? Damn poor companions.

His Belle wouldn't look at him anyway, prickly moralist that she was. He was a red-blooded Englishman in his estimation, a depraved libertine in hers, in either identity. She never wanted to see him again. He never wanted anything more than to have her beside him, forever.

"Floyd, another bottle."

"Miss Cristabel, Miss Cristabel, come quick! It's Mac, and he's all beat up!"

"Mac? Oh, Mac, what happened to you? Your poor eye, and your lip! Here, sit down. Fanny, go get wet cloths and whatever else you can find."

Major MacDermott staggered to a seat in the parlor, leaning on Cristabel. "My word, Mac, did Nick do this to you?" she asked. "I didn't believe he was that dangerous! I'll have to go to Bow Street after all. We'll write out a warrant and have him arrested and—"

"What kind of clunch do you think I am?" Mac mumbled painfully through his split lip. "No twiddling little flat could have done this to me."

"Footpads? Were you set on by a gang of thieves in broad daylight?"

"Arrgh. It was your bloody viscount."

"Lord Winstoke? When you told him about us? I mean, when you told him there was nothing to tell?"

"He hit me before I could say anything."

"But you told him?"

"Yeah, then he hit me again. Said he would have killed me if he thought otherwise."

"Oh dear. Mac, does this mean you'll have to call him out? Will there be a duel?"

With only one eye still open, he fixed it on Miss Swann like she'd grown another head. "If I wanted to die, you peahen, I'd go back to the wars. What would you have me do, challenge him over the honor of his own ladybird?"

So she hit him.

What a violent, hostile shrew Cristabel was turning out to be! She did not like it, or understand it. In her whole adult life, the worst she'd done was kick the occasional chair leg for getting in her way, and once she had pinched a student at Miss Meadow's for bringing a toad to church. Now, in less than twenty-four hours, she had spilled punch in a gentleman's lap, poured wash water over another one's feet, and even struck someone in anger! She could not remember such furious thoughts or such physical outpourings of uncontrolled emotions.

Moderation, that had been the rule. Placid, decorous, and boring, the Golden Mean was more comfortable than this turmoil of indignation and upset, this tightrope between hope and despair off which she was constantly falling. Passionate outbursts were unseemly and unproductive, although Miss Swann had felt a touch of satisfaction—she was only human. But they had to stop. She had to control her thoughts and her actions, put aside all those foolish notions of a Grand Passion and get back to an ordinary, crisis-free existence.

Hadn't she improved the house in just one day? And hadn't she already found a respectable lodger? Then she could certainly bring a halt to this emotional drivel, and start using her God-given good sense.

Therefore Miss Swann promptly changed into her ugly but sturdy flannel nightgown, brushed her hair precisely one hundred strokes, climbed into her bed—and cried herself to sleep.

Sleep was hard in coming and full of dreams. If Cristabel's dreams betrayed her finer principles and her new resolutions both, well, no one could control their sleeping thoughts.

Lord Winstoke was in her night fantasy, not surprising since she had fallen asleep with him on her mind. They were dancing the waltz, as light as air, spinning and twirling effortlessly, while they stared into each other's eyes. She fell deeper and deeper into the gray depths of his gaze, still floating, as if on clouds. Then he moved closer and pressed his lips to hers, as tender as sunlight, as soft as a pillow. They danced and drifted, lost in an endless kiss that became more insistent, stealing her breath away. They were spinning faster, too fast. She couldn't get enough air. She was afraid!

"Stop, stop!" she shouted, and woke up suffocating, with a pillow over her face! She thrashed wildly and hit something soft enough to force an *"oosh"* from her attacker and a momentary loosening of the pillow's pressure. Cristabel managed to scream before the downward push was returned, but she'd also taken a deep breath, so

struck out with more force. There was no way any one
man was going to dodge two arms and two legs while
using both of his own hands to hold her and the pillow, so
the would-be murderer was not having an easy time of it
either. The sound of footsteps on the stair and shouting,
worried voices convinced him to leave before the job was
finished, or he was.

Cristabel threw off the pillow and jumped out of bed,
following the crashing sounds of the intruder finding his
way to the front door in the darkness.

Marie stood with a candle at the top of the stairs—and
a gentleman caller, with a pistol, pulling on his pants.
Cristabel required a moment to absorb that vignette, and
almost missed seeing Nick Blass scamper through the
front door.

She leaned against the wall to catch her breath and
slow her heart's frantic pounding. Fanny and Boy, both in
nightshirts, came tearing up the back steps. Fanny was
wielding a metal soup ladle, Boy a butcher knife.

"We was just practicing our letters, ma'am," Fanny
replied to her scowl. "Really, we was." She kicked Boy,
who was grinning, and changed the subject. "It was Nick,
wasn't it, Miss Cristabel? I knew he was no good. It were
those eyes, just like Uncle Lewis's, what got hanged
for—"

"Not now, Fanny. Boy, get dressed and fetch the
watch. I'm sure Nick got away, but maybe they can find
him."

"But what happened, Miss Cristabel? How'd Nick get
in?"

"With his own key, I expect!" Cristabel said with
much disgust. "My wits have gone begging lately. We'll
need the locksmith and the Runners after all. If they can-

not protect me, at least they can advise us about things like that."

"You're calling in Bow Street? Good grief, Marie, they cannot find me here! Where's my jacket, find my boots!" Lord Chauncey Radway was waving the pistol around in a frenzy, putting Cristabel in worse jeopardy than she was in from Nick's pillow.

Then young Mr. Haynes wandered down the stairs from the attics in his shirtsleeves, a quill in his hand.

"I say, Miss Swann, you promised this was a quiet establishment where I could get my writing done."

"I'm dreadfully sorry, Mr. Haynes. I hadn't intended on being murdered in my bed."

"It won't happen again, will it?"

"I sincerely hope not!"

"Good, good. Otherwise I'd have to move, you know." And he drifted back up the stairs.

"Who was that?" Lord Radway wanted to know, struggling into his jacket with Marie's assistance.

"Just the new boarder, love, a nice lad who writes for the papers," Marie told him.

"A reporter? My God, I've got to get out of here! If this ever got back to my wife . . ." He grabbed his boots out of Marie's hands and raced down the stairs, calling over his shoulder, "I'll try to come by next month when I am in town on business again. You'll have to let me know if it's safe to call."

"But, but what about the place of my own we were going to look for this visit?"

"Sorry, sweets. I cannot chance the notoriety. The wife's breeding, you know. I can't upset her at a time like this. The heir and all." He managed to get out of the door faster than Nick had.

Marie fell to the ground wailing. "He's abandoned me!

I've got no place and no savings and I'll be out on the street! What am I going to do? I'll starve to death, I'll throw myself in the river, I'll—"

"You'll stop working yourself into hysteria this instant!" Cristabel demanded, having seen quite enough tantrums among the girls at school. "If you don't, I'll throw this jug of water on you, so help me I will," she said, pulling flowers out of a vase and advancing up the stairs, totally out of patience. You'd think Marie was the one nearly killed by a lunatic. "He is not worth your tears. Good riddance to bad rubbish, if you ask me. And you will *not* be out on the street. We'll work something out, I swear we will. Please Marie, please don't cry."

It was too late as the other girl was already blubbering into her sleeve, but Cristabel could pick out a few phrases, such as "Skinny shanks," and "wet kisses."

"Really, Miss Swann, I must protest this continued disturbance. I cannot think, and if I cannot think, I cannot write, and if I cannot write—"

"I know, you cannot pay the rent. We'll try very hard, Mr. Haynes. The, ah, disturbance should be over now. Here, Fanny, you take Marie up to her room. And stay there!"

"I think she could use some tea. My mum always said—"

"Very well, I'm sure I could use some also. But there is to be no more visiting with Boy in the middle of the night. Do you understand? Look where it got Marie."

"Oh, I wouldn't take money, Miss Cristabel. That'd be wrong. Boy and me, we're just friends."

Miss Swann sank into a chair, her head between her hands, and sighed. Fanny scooted, dragging the limp Marie after, leaving Cristabel alone in the hallway. Alone! She jumped up and locked the door. Fine lot of

good that had done her, about as much good as her other
defenders. Now that she had time to think about it, where
was the guard dog Boy mentioned? She never heard so
much as a bark. Her kitten would have done better.

The other protection was coming down the stairs now,
fully dressed, buckling on his sword belt. "What's all the
ruckus?" Mac asked.

The night watchman was no help; the charlie was a
stooped old man with little hair and less teeth and a mis-
placed levity, in Cristabel's opinion.

"You complaining about a man in your bedroom?" he
cackled. "That's a new one for this place, dearie. What's
the matter? He wouldn't pay up?"

"He tried to kill me, you jackanapes!"

"Ar-ar. And you expect me to go chasing after some
swell that likes to play rough? You got to get yourself a
protector, girl."

"It was the pro—that is, the person who attacked me
was a former employee."

"Changin' horses midstream, eh?" He chortled in
Mac's direction. "That's the ticket." Then he got a better
look at Mac's battered face. "Can't say as how I'd lay my
blunt on this one. 'Course I ain't seen the other fella. No
matter, us civil servants are paid to watch out for honest
folks, not be wet-nursin' you baby dolls, ar-ar."

So Cristabel made Major MacDermott escort her to
Bow Street. She dressed in one of her new gowns, but
carefully buttoned her heavy old woolen cloak over it.
The officer in charge was a great deal more respectful, if
only a bit more helpful.

"It's like this, ma'am. The Runners are an independent
lot. They work hardest when the case offers the biggest
reward. I don't suppose . . . No, I didn't think so," he said

regretfully, eyeing her shabby cape. "In that case, they'll keep an eye out for this Blass person, but not much else, I'm afraid."

He went on to recommend that she move, which was an impossibility, of course, as she owned the boarding-house. In that case, the officer suggested, she might take in a soldier at reduced rent, to help guard the premises. Cristabel sniffed disdainfully, thinking of Mac, waiting outside where no one could see his black eye. The Runner got the idea she wouldn't let a man in the house. Too bad, too, for if she was dressed up a bit . . .

"Then, ma'am, I can only advise you to get a big dog and a pistol. A lot of housebreakers are discouraged by the barking, and at least you are warned in time to get the gun. I don't usually like to see ladies with weapons like that. Too often they shoot their husbands, coming home from a late night at the clubs, you know, thinking he's a burglar. At least that's what they say, the widows, that is. But in your case . . ."

In her case it sounded like an excellent idea. Mac should be good for that; at least he could teach her how to shoot. Not that she would ever have to fire the pistol, actually. Cristabel was certain that pocket-bully Nick Blass would be frightened by the very sight of a weapon in her hand. She would be.

Chapter Fourteen

The next day brought a lot of changes to 15 Sullivan Street, a house that had already seen more than its share of comings and goings over the years. The first was new locks.

"Boy, before you go to fetch back a locksmith, I'd like to see this watchdog we have. I didn't hear it bark last night or anything."

"He's real mean though," was her answer, on the way down to the kitchens. A big, black, mangy cur lifted its head to snarl at her when she bent to inspect it. He was mean all right.

"Are you sure the animal is safe?"

"Sure. Feed him and give him a soft place to sleep upstairs, and he'll guard his territory and his next meal."

So Cristabel gathered the scraps under Boy's direction and the beast's yellow-eyed stare and pushed the bowl closer to the animal with her foot, saying "Nice doggy," and feeling stupid. He was not a nice doggy. He was not even a male doggy, Cristabel could see now. He, she, rather, was also flea-bitten and filthy.

"Do you think she could have a bath if I am to have her in my bedroom?"

Boy looked doubtful, scratching his head. Cristabel wondered if he was considering whether the dog would

hate the bath and bite, or whether Miss Swann was crazy
to worry over a little dirt and insect life. "I know," she advised, "I bet the dog would do just fine if you got in the
tub with her."

"But I was cleaned up yesterday, mopping the steps."

"Marie said your new shirt would be ready this afternoon. You wouldn't want to put that on until you've had
a proper bath, would you? Here, I'll fetch the soap and
some towels. You set the water on to heat. . . ."

Boy made more fuss than the dog, which, having
eaten, only wanted to sleep by the fire. Boy also came out
of the tub improved; the old bitch stayed mangy and
mean. Cristabel led the dog upstairs, at a distance, by
trailing pieces of muffin. She took up that stained brown
dress she'd worn to polish the brass, the one she left to be
used for rags, and neatly folded it into a mat at the foot of
her bed.

"Here, Dog," she called, that being all Boy had used as
name for the animal, naturally. "No, I cannot refer to you
as Dog. You shall be . . . Meadowlark, yes Meadowlark,
for Miss Meadow, a fierce old bitch if there ever was one.
Good doggy, here's your bed." She put the rest of the
muffin down and gingerly reached out to pat the grizzled
old head.

Meadowlark swallowed the muffin, suffered the pat,
pawed the dress into a lumpier nest, and collapsed onto it,
fast asleep, having wind.

Cristabel left in a rush to send Boy off on his errand.
When the dog never even stirred at the locksmith's presence, Boy told her, "Front door ain't his territory."

Cristabel did enough growling herself at the locksmith, who charged double for coming out on an emer-
gency, it being Sunday, so Boy's explanation seemed
reasonable enough. She knew as much about dogs as Boy

knew about Dorian tetrachords and diatonic intervals. She was going to learn a lot more about them a lot sooner than she planned.

"You brought me a what?"

"It's a foxhound pup. Isn't he a beauty? Fellow I went to for your pistol had a litter of them."

"I can't hear you, Mac. Tell the dog to be quiet."

"You don't want him to be quiet, Belle. You need a good loud dog to wake you up if there's an intruder."

"More likely he'll wake the whole neighborhood, all night. Besides, if he barks all the time, how will I know if something is wrong?"

"He won't keep it up, he's just excited. See, he's quieter already."

"That's because his mouth is full. He's chewing on the curtains! Make him stop, Mac."

"Here, sir, down. Down I say, not the tassel on my boots, damn you. Don't worry, Belle, it's just high spirits. He'll make you a fine watchdog."

"He's making a fine mess on the rug."

The new dog, who came with the appellation Beau, was excused to the tiny bare spot behind the house, where he could guard the rear entry. Tied to the kitchen stair post, he could stay there until someone, Mac or Boy, had time to teach him house manners. Boy found an old bone to keep him quiet, meantime, although Cristabel vowed to see the animal sent off to a better home in the country as soon as possible. Any country.

"Bringing me the dog was really thoughtful, Lyle, but did you get the pistol?"

"As sweet as can stare!"

The weapon didn't look sweet at all, to Miss Swann. It looked cold and deadly, heavy and intimidating. Its pearl inlays would have appealed more as silverware handles.

She touched it with the same enthusiasm she'd shown patting Meadowlark. (Beau hadn't stood still long enough to be petted.)

"The only thing is, Belle, we've got nowhere to practice. I mean, you can't fire it in the house, and out here the yard is too small to set up a target, and you can't just waltz into Manton's Shooting Gallery like a gent could, so I don't know what's to do. Maybe we could rent a carriage and go for a ride in the country."

And drop off the dog, she thought, but didn't say. She also didn't say the beast might make a perfect target for one of the irate neighbors if it didn't shut up. "That's fine, Lyle," she did say. "If you just show me how to load it and what to do if I should want to fire it, that will be enough for today. I think the weapon is more to give me confidence than anything else, you see. Just knowing I have it and can wave it around makes me feel more secure."

That reasoning made no sense whatsoever to Major MacDermott, who often carried a pistol and a knife in his boot, along with his sword and the skean dhu of his regimentals. He demonstrated how to load the thing anyway, then let her try. He held it out and sighted down the barrel, then let her try that. Of course, the nodcock had bought her a showy piece with a hair trigger that he'd neglected to mention. The gun went off, defoliating a neighbor's shrub, setting Beau to howling, and bringing Mr. Haynes outside to complain.

"Miss Swann, this is the outside of enough. Hammering, barking, gunshots—on a Sunday, no less! My one day free when I could get a great deal accomplished, after church of course. I am afraid I cannot stay here any longer."

Mac started to explain that the house was quieter than

it had been for years, but Cristabel silenced him with a glare. Taking Mr. Haynes by the arm, she led him back indoors. "All is quiet now, you see? I was about to go to church myself. It's just across the square. Will you join me?"

"What about that dog? He looks like he's going to keep on barking."

"Oh, no he won't," said Miss Swann, tossing the dog one of the leather gloves Mac had removed in order to explain the fine points of the pistol. "Thank you, Major," she added sweetly.

After church Cristabel and Marie, who was too distraught to attend services, held a conference, the end result of which was another sign in the front windows of the house. This one read: FINE DRESSMAKING AND ALTERATIONS BY MLLE. MARIE. If there were many more signs in those poor windows, no light would get in the house at all.

"It won't work," Marie whimpered. "I know it won't. No one will come, and I'll have no rent money or food or—"

"It's bound to be successful. There are so many ladies who cannot afford the Bond Street modistes, they'll be happy to find someone reasonable, closer to home. And meanwhile you can make Fanny's and Boy's uniforms, finish the green silk gown you started for me, and not worry about the rent. It's not like there's no space. We can even take the room next to yours upstairs and make it into a real showroom, or a sewing studio, so you can have try-on alcoves and all. Fanny will help, I'm sure. As for food, we can all take potluck together."

"And you really think I can make enough money to support myself?"

"You can certainly try, can't you?"

"And maybe save enough for a dowry?"

"I don't see why not."

Marie snuffled into her hanky. "I don't know how to thank you. I don't think I ever can."

"You can start by not being such a watering pot. Please don't get tear stains on the green silk. I don't have time to embroider any more butterflies."

This eventful day then saw one of Cristabel's prayers answered: boarders. Real, honest, paying boarders. A young newlywed couple by the name of Todd took Mac's suite. They wished to stay in Kensington while their first house was under construction a few blocks away. The Douglas sisters, two genteel spinsters, claimed an upstairs bed-sitter, and a Mrs. Flint, a prepossessing lady of a certain age, had come to London to have her wardrobe refurbished now that she was out of mourning. Mr. Flint must have been vastly successful at whatever he did, to judge by his widow's jewels, baggage, and the number of servants she wished housed in the attic level. She did not like the noise and dirt of the city itself so was pleased with quiet accommodations. She was also pleased with Cristabel's gown and hired Marie on the spot. Unfortunately, she was not pleased with the remaining upper suites, so Cristabel volunteered her own rooms, at a higher price, naturally, and payment in advance—for the season. Two hundred pounds! She was finally a real landlady! And a music teacher, again. A turbaned dowager arrived with two young ladies in tow, causing Mr. Haynes to rethink demanding his advance rent monies returned; he could not stay in such a chaotic environment. One look at the twin sugarplums sitting mumchance on the chintz-covered sofa, however, had him reconsidering. He returned upstairs to his muse, inspired.

It remained only for Cristabel to move her belongings to the two rooms across from Marie's, regretting mostly the library downstairs, even with its still-empty shelves. She made the change with help from Fanny and Boy, accompanied by her latest, least welcomed new boarder, another dog. Mrs. Flint, it seemed, never traveled without her bowlegged, barrel-bodied and black-faced pug, who wheezed with every breath. None of which stopped the midget moonling from immediately falling passionately in love with Meadowlark, the noisome bitch who could only be coaxed up to Cristabel's new bedroom by the offer of a mutton shank. The treat pleased the flea hound into wagging her tail, which whapped the diminutive Don Juan seven ways to Sunday, knocking Pug back down the stairs. Two hundred pounds could buy a lot of books, however, and a lot of music lessons, and a lot of lavender water for Meadowlark. For two hundred pounds she could even tolerate the wheezes and whines of the rat-sized Romeo.

The final, and perchance greatest, surprise of the day came in the form of a letter from Captain Chase, of all people. The shock wasn't just that he'd finally remembered common courtesy enough to inquire as to her welfare; the jolt was his kindness and humility in asking her pardon for the unfortunate contretemps. If there was anything she recalled about the captain, it was not his humility! A more arrogant, overbearing—no, she wouldn't start.

The letter was charming, in fact, written in terms almost of friendship. She felt that she knew him, or he knew her, to trust her with private thoughts, in hopes of understanding.

He had been ill, he wrote, and sick with worry over what was to become of him. Having recently lost his ship and his men, and being set adrift himself, he could not at the time accept responsibility for her, as any gentleman would have done. He begged her forgiveness and asked if there was anything he could do to assist her now, however belatedly. Did she require additional monies? Was the property situated conveniently for her? Could he offer the services of the messenger waiting for a reply, his man Sparling, or himself, now that he was no longer incapacitated? Could she forgive him?

It really seemed to matter to the man, Cristabel sensed, with wonder. She sent Marie down to tell Sparling there would be no immediate reply; she needed time to think.

"Thank him very warmly for me and for his offer of assistance." Mr. Sparling was even then helping the men carry in that mountain of baggage Mrs. Flint deemed a few "necessities."

"Why don't you take him to the kitchen and fix him some tea?" She didn't want the boarders to see Marie all red-eyed and droopy while the girl still looked more like a jilted lover than a fashionable modiste. At least Cristabel needn't worry over anyone encountering Mac, who still resembled the loser of a barroom brawl, not when there was work to be done and better impressions to be made at a later time. Miss Swann had seen that light of pound notes gleam in Mac's eye, the one that wasn't purple and puffed closed, when she'd described the nabob's widow.

Meantime, she had to respond to Captain Chase's note. But how? Should she complain or admit her difficulties to him and accept his offer of aid? An offer, incidentally, which came now that things were on their way to being resolved.

Men! she thought, pacing between her new small bedroom and her adjoining, small sitting room, stepping over the drowsing Meadowlark every circuit, frowning at the drooling pug. Bah!

There was that nodcock Lyle, an empty rattle with the smile of a cherub and the heart of a cardsharp, only out for money, of which she had none to spare anyway. Lord Winstoke—she hadn't thought about him for at least ten minutes—was only after her virtue, which she was absolutely, positively, rock-hard, and immovably in no danger of losing, she hoped. Now here was Captain Chase, that old reprobate, finally acting like a gentleman and wanting to be her friend. Who was a girl to trust? Herself, that was who!

Chapter Fifteen

"I must beg your pardon, also," Cristabel finally wrote to Captain Chase, "for my deplorable conduct on that unfortunate afternoon. I can only plead a minor indisposition and the fatigue of the journey as excuses for my lapse, along with dismay at my circumstances, caused, I must assure you, by my own rash actions.

"You must not think for one instant that I hold you responsible for my welfare, despite your kind offer. You have already been more than gracious in deeding me this property. After an awkward beginning, due again to my inexperience, the house is becoming successful, enough so that I may thankfully return your loan. Please accept my heartfelt gratitude and congratulations on your return to health."

Cristabel had some trouble with the close: Respectfully yours? But did she respect him? Your servant? Never! She settled on "Sincerely," but tacked on an invitation to take tea some afternoon, at his convenience, out of conscience and curiosity.

She wondered if the captain really was as civilized as his letter indicated or if a secretary did the writing for the savage. She would also like to know what he looked like, without all the bandages. She recalled him being tall, nearly as tall as Viscount Winstoke, but not as broad. He must have dark hair, from the stubble on his chin and the curls on his chest, which image she hastily consigned to the furthest reaches of her mind. Mostly she remembered the voice, gruff and booming, that would rattle the very windows on the front parlor if he ever came to call. He wouldn't, of course, not that toplofty libertine. He would be too busy at his debauchery for such a tame pastime as tea with a "self-righteous spinster." She unfortunately remembered a lot of his words, too.

"Tea!" he shouted, sending a footman and two maids scurrying off to the kitchens. "How in bloody hell can I go there as Captain Chase?"

"In your dress uniform?" Jonas Sparling offered, which only got him a darkling look and the offending letter waved in his face.

"Blast, what a coil. And you say there's something havey-cavey going on there?"

"Aye, something's not shipshape, but Miss Marie didn't say what."

"Miss Marie?"

"Aye, she's the trim little galley what does the sewing over there, like I told you. Sad eyes, she has, but a friendly smile and the shape of a mermaid."

"You better watch yourself, man, you know about the women there."

"So she ain't on her maiden voyage, m'lord. That just proves she's seaworthy, if you get my drift."

Winstoke did. "Then you won't mind calling there and keeping an eye on things for me till I can straighten out this mare's nest."

"Be my pleasure, Cap'n."

"Not too much pleasure, Sparling. Don't get us into deeper waters."

"I thought we was already on the rocks, Cap'n, sir."

Just then the footman entered with a tray. "What the devil is that?" Winstoke thundered.

"Tea, my lord, like you ordered."

"Tea? Why is everybody suddenly trying to drown me in tea? I am trying to think, by George, not cure a cold. Get it out of here."

Winstoke tapped his chin with Cristabel's letter. "I wish I knew what kind of trouble she was having."

"All Marie would say was the watch wasn't much help; that's why they had a parcel of mongrel watchdogs around. None of them worth a maggoty sea biscuit, if you ask me."

"You'll have to go back. . . . Let me think."

By the next morning, Winstoke had a course of action. He sent Sparling off to Kensington to return the hundred pounds, which was a gift, not a loan, his note said, and he also wrote, regretfully, that business would keep him from accepting her kind invitation to tea. The captain sent a bouquet of roses along with Sparling and the note and, since he was already at the flower sellers, had the shop boy deliver a nosegay of violets to the house on Sullivan Street, signed "Yrs., Winstoke." A good commander always had a second plan of attack, and took any port in a storm.

That's how the next stage of Winstoke's campaign went: Cristabel would return the money, he'd send it back with Sparling, tucked in sheet music for the harp, inside a box of bonbons, under the cover of a book. It wasn't a loan, it was a gift. If she wrote that she couldn't accept a gift of that magnitude, for propriety's sake, he sent it back, for his conscience's sake. Now it wasn't a gift, it was repayment of a moral debt. She had a conscience, too; he had honor. She had honor; he had persistence. It was all lighthearted and charming, especially to Marie, who smiled a great deal now. As for Cristabel, the peripatetic hundred-pound note gave her a chance at playful banter, a silly challenge, a time to get her mind off Viscount Winstoke. Captain Chase's roses were decorating the parlor, but Winstoke's violets were in a vase next to her bed. Neither one called.

She did not care, she told herself, that he—Winstoke, of course, not Chase—had believed her declaration about never wanting to see him again. It mattered not a whit, she insisted, that he finally realized she was a lady and now wasn't interested at all. Then why, she wondered, if she couldn't give a fare-thee-well farthing, were her days so dismal, her nights so empty? She gave herself a mental shake and practiced a hollow social smile for the boarders . . . until she went downstairs for tea. There he was, sitting at perfect ease, chatting with Mrs. Flint and the Douglas sisters. No, not Captain Chase, whom she might have expected, but the viscount, looking even more devastatingly handsome than she remembered. Her heart was smiling, a warm glow singing inside her; he'd come. He cared. But what if he was only here to repeat his improper advances? What if he offended the boarders with his murky morals?

"What are you doing here?" she hissed as he jumped up at her entrance.

"You invited me for tea, remember?"

"I never did! I told you I never wanted to see you again."

"Oh, I must have been thinking of someone else."

"You have windmills in your head, my lord, and—"

"I know. Amazing, isn't it?" And he treated her to that rare smile that started on one side of his mouth and widened to light up his eyes. She had to get him out of here, before her knees gave out.

As if reading her mind—or her nervous glance at the tittering Douglas sisters—the viscount declared it a perfect day for a drive, unless Miss Swann preferred taking tea with her lovely guests. The formidable Mrs. Flint snorted, and Cristabel ran out for her cloak and bonnet which a grinning Fanny, in her neat new uniform, already had in hand.

There was nothing for it but that Cristabel take the arm his lordship held out to her. She did *not* have to return his triumphant smile.

The curricle was shiny black with gold trim and had a crest on the door. The tiger was a young lad who jumped up behind as soon as Winstoke had the reins. The horses were matched bays, sleek and eager. And the passengers were—Well, the passengers made less noise than the well-greased carriage wheels. The viscount was concentrating too hard to make conversation, trying to remember Perry's lessons about getting the new team through the traffic and repeating in his mind the speech he'd been rehearsing, for when they reached the park. Then he could hand over the blasted reins and take Miss Swann in his arms as he longed to do. For her part, Cristabel didn't know why his lordship had come, why he was glowering at the horses, or why she was feeling trembly just from his nearness on the narrow seat.

This was absurd. Boy would have more discourse. "Thank you for the violets," she said, at the same moment he said, "Thank you for coming." They smiled. He complimented her on her pretty gown; she admired his new prowess with the ribbons; they agreed it was one of the loveliest days so far this season. They smiled during the long pauses. The tiger shook his head in disgust.

"How is it you never mentioned you were a school teacher?" the viscount asked when there was an empty stretch of road.

Cristabel was still pondering why he had invited her out, with a tiger up behind for propriety's sake. "What was that? Oh, Miss Meadow. How did you learn about that?"

"Uh, one of the boarders must have mentioned something about it. You never did." If there was the slightest bit of rancor, that if Miss Swann had been more forthcoming, he'd not have landed them in such a bumblebroth, Winstoke hid it in threading his carriage through the traffic at the park gates.

"It was not a particularly pleasant time for me; I suppose that's why I never talked about it. My life in the vicarage in earlier years was much happier."

"You never specifically mentioned a vicarage either, you know." His mouth twisted.

"I didn't? Are you sure?"

"Quite."

"No matter, Miss Meadow's Academy for Young Ladies was nothing I wish to dwell on. It's like your period in the Army, I'd guess."

Now was the perfect opportunity to correct her, to tell Miss Swann that it was the Navy, not the Army, where he'd been, and been wounded. Near blinded, in fact. He'd seen ample evidence of his Belle's temper, however, and wasn't about to chance it, not in front of half the *ton* out for their promenade. She'd flay him alive, without a doubt. No, much better to go as planned, find a secluded spot and make his speech. Then, he thought with a smile, when she was in his arms and rosy with his kisses, then he could confess his identity. He was not a coward; he wasn't a clunch, either. "Shall we get down and walk?" he asked.

Cristabel wasn't craven either, she just had a good memory about another day in the park, and her own less-than-proper response to being alone with his lordship. "No, thank you. It's such a pleasure seeing things from this altitude."

Winstoke frowned. Then his brow cleared and he told the tiger to get down for a bit, they were just going to walk the horses over to that stand of trees to cool the beasts. At least there would be privacy.

The viscount took a deep breath. "Miss Swann," he began his prepared oration. "Belle, there is a lot about me that you don't know and some, I'm afraid, you wouldn't like." The horses were ambling along under the trees, so he relaxed his grip on the reins and turned to Cristabel. She looked so dashed alluring with her face turned up to him expectantly, sweetly, and the tiniest bit cautiously. Her tongue darted out to lick her lower lip nervously and Winstoke forgot all the words he was supposed to say. "Oh God, Belle, you are the world to me! I have to have you by my side, dearest. Please, please let me care for you. Come home with me and—"

Cristabel heard *care* for you, as in place you in my keeping, and *home*, as in a bachelor's rooms. What she didn't hear were words of love, or doing the great honor, or the rest of his sentence, which was, "Come home with me and meet my mother." She jumped to her feet and turned to climb down from the carriage, which saved her

life, for what she next heard was the loud crack of a gunshot.

The horses heard it, too, and felt the bullet whine just
over their heads, and they panicked. Cristabel was
slammed back into her seat by the sudden lurch forward
of the curricle, and Winstoke grabbed up the slack in the
reins. He was too late, for in his moment of inexperienced
hesitation the bays had the bits between their teeth and
were bolting toward the crowded carriage path. Winstoke
sawed on the ribbons, his shoulders straining, and finally
succeeded in turning the horses back to the trees away
from the groups of people who were already screaming,
doing the frightened animals no more good than his
whoas. Then the carriage grazed a tree trunk and slewed
around behind the horses to aim crosswise toward another. Instead of hitting broadside, the wheel caught and
wedged the curricle in tight against the bole, stopping
horses, carriage, and Miss Swann in an instant. Lord
Winstoke, however, holding onto the reins instead of the
carriage sides like Cristabel, went flying off the seat at
the sudden halt. He missed the tree by mere inches and
landed with a dust-raising splat right between the horses.
The vicious, unpredictable, immense horses, Cristabel
thought in horror. She got off the carriage almost as
quickly as Winstoke had done, running around to dodge
between the flailing hooves and drag his unconscious
body to safety.

Of course, the horses were placidly grazing by then.
They were good-natured beasts, selected by the viscount's friend Adler for just that quality, and had carefully stepped around their master to reach the greener
grass as soon as they realized that forward progress was
impossible, as well as unnecessary.

Merely winded, the viscount had already crawled out

of hoof range, but he let Cristabel help prop him against the tree while he caught his breath. In fact, he might let her cradle his head and weep her agonized outpourings over him forever, rather than face the ignominy of the crowds he could see rushing to their aid. Zounds, some hero he was, with grass stains on his shirt front. And it could have been her, his precious Belle, thrown out of the curricle—and all because of his stupid pride. He could drive that pair as well as hedgehogs could sing, but he had wanted to show off for her. He might have gotten her killed instead. He groaned.

"Please don't die! Oh please don't die!" Cristabel sobbed, knowing she would see that picture of him sailing out of the curricle a hundred times in her nightmares, knowing suddenly that if he died she may as well die, too. It didn't matter that he was a rake, with all the scruples of a slug. She loved him. She didn't know how it happened, or what she could do about it, or why Cupid played such stupid tricks on people, but she loved him. Just don't let him be hurt, she prayed, and held him closer.

"I'd be less likely to perish, dear heart, if I could breathe," he told her with a smile and a wink. She dropped her arms and jumped up. He got to his feet, a little more slowly, and softly brushed a tear from her cheek. "You do care," he whispered as the tiger and others ran up to them. "Everything will be fine, you'll see."

He could not say more, not with so many people examining the horses and hauling the curricle free, or later, driving home at an embarrassingly slow pace, his hat missing, his clothing rumpled, the tiger mutinous behind. Cristabel was silent, too, hoping the viscount would not renew his shameful offer, not now, when her love was new and her heart ached to share the discovery.

It was the tiger who mumbled and muttered the whole way back to Kensington. He didn't care if it wasn't his place to find fault with his betters, deuce if he'd work for such a cow-handed fiddler. The viscount couldn't drive worth a tinker's damn, and he sure as hell was no better at courting the ladies, to judge from how far apart the two sat, stone-faced and still.

None of them gave a moment's thought to the gunshot.

Chapter Sixteen

How could she choose between love and self-respect? To be a fallen woman in the eyes of the world—and in her own mind—or to live the rest of her life as a lonely, loveless old maid? Maybe there was nothing wrong with giving one's love where one's heart led. Certainly Marie and even little Fanny saw nothing amiss in following their desires. Then again, maybe there was a higher goal, as Cristabel remembered her parents' marriage and their deep abiding affection built on trust and love and respect.

If he truly loved her, he wouldn't ask. If he did ask, though, if that was the only way to keep him near, to share the warmth of his smile, to rid her stomach of the knot of dread that she might never see him again, what then? Cristabel didn't know, so she was happy to throw herself into her boarders' plans for them all to attend the opera the next evening.

It was to be Mrs. Flint's first social appearance in colors, the Douglas sisters' first visit to the opera, and one of the few times the Todds appeared out of their rooms at all. There was a great flurry of selecting just the right combinations of fans, feathers, finery. Cristabel took it on herself to go match some ribbons, avoiding most of the hurly-burly, and Winstoke's next visit.

"Your viscount called," Marie informed Cristabel on

her return. "Dressed to the nines he was, too. Too bad you missed him," she added, amused to note Cristabel's discomfiture. The two of them were a pair of lovesick loobies, if she knew anything.

"I told him you were going to the opera tonight along with Mac and the renters. Guess what? He's going, too. He said he would visit your box during the break."

So Cristabel went upstairs and emptied *her* wardrobe to select the perfect outfit.

The choice didn't take long: the just-completed green silk was perfect, simple and elegant. The neckline was filled in, over Marie's protests, with a triangle of white lace, the gown's only ornamentation. White gloves and a white ostrich feather sewn to a green headband completed the ensemble—hours before it was time to dress. Marie suggested a nap, but Cristabel was too fidgety. Fresh air and exercise, that's what she needed. Fresh air would do her room good, too, especially with her gown hanging on the wardrobe door, if she wasn't to smell like an old dog tonight. She opened the windows and dragged Meadowlark down the stairs, Pug following, of course.

Fanny thought it would be a good idea to get the young hound out back some exercise, too, then maybe it wouldn't keep chewing on the fence posts or howling. Naturally Boy would have to come along, being the only one who could control the untrained pup. Fanny's hopeful grin had nothing to do with it; Cristabel was feeling guilty enough about the dog and the neighbors.

It was not the rambunctious foxhound that started all the trouble. It wasn't even the growly Meadowlark, disgruntled at having her rest disturbed. It was the caper-witted little pug, who felt he had to defend his ladylove from the inquisitive sniffs of a debonair poodle. The poodle was attached, via a silken lead, to a foppish young gentleman's perfumed wrist.

The barking sent a squirrel flying for the trees, and Beau after, baying *view halloo* for all Kensington to hear. Boy went hollering after, but the stupid dog didn't even recollect its own name in the joy of the hunt, if it heard Boy's yells at all. The dandy was wrapped in the poodle's leash like a Christmas goose, teetering on his yellow high-heeled shoes and screeching. Pug was yapping just out of reach of the now-irate poodle's jaws while Fanny added her squeals, running in circles after Pug, around the poodle and the fribble, like a very peculiar Maypole dance. And Meadowlark? The nasty old bitch had met her match in an old lady feeding the squirrels from a sack of bread. The two were engaged in a furious, high-pitched tug-of-war over the bag, with the old dog snarling like a hellhound, and the old woman punctuating her strident shouts with whaps of her umbrella on Meadowlark's thick head. Two nursemaids decided to scream, setting the infants in the prams to caterwauling, and a small boy blew his wooden whistle, just for the excitement of the thing.

Cristabel made a dash toward the fop and bent down to scoop up Pug, just as the sound of a gunshot was heard.

It worked. Everyone was so shocked by the sudden sharp boom that there was silence, and a moment's stunned immobility. Just enough time for Cristabel to get a firm grip on Pug, and another on Fanny's wrist, and drag both away. Boy lunged for Beau's collar and hauled him off, and Meadowlark was already on her way home, tail between her legs but the sack of bread in her teeth.

Trying to ignore the frayed tempers behind her, Cristabel hurried her party out of the park, remembering to call a "Thank you" over her shoulder to whatever gentleman had the foresight to fire his pistol to end the melee.

"Exercise did you the world of good," Marie told her. "Your cheeks are nice and pink. Are you sure you didn't overdo it, though?" she worried as Cristabel sank into a chair in the parlor.

"Oh no," Cristabel gasped. "I'll be fine in a moment. I wouldn't miss this evening for the world."

"Good, good. You missed another caller, though. Not a caller actually, a messenger. That nice Mr. Sparling your Captain Chase sends here for lunch every day. He brought this."

This was a letter and a package. "How strange," Cristabel said when she had read the single sheet. "Captain Chase writes that he came upon a box of my uncle's papers and discovered that Lord Harwood had left a Swann family heirloom in pawn, for a loan. He used that silly hundred pounds to redeem it. Do you think that sounds right?"

"If he says it's yours, it's yours. You can't dispute the word of a gentleman. Go on, Belle, open it."

"Oh," Cristabel sighed, uncovering a strand of perfectly matched pearls gleaming on the velvet. "Do you really think I can wear them?"

"Who else? They should have come to you anyway. That captain did just what's proper. I wonder if he'll attend the opera tonight to see you wearing them." Marie hoped so, so she could hear about him later. Miss Swann and her suitors could put on a better show than the opera.

"What's that? Oh, I doubt the captain cares for opera." Opera dancers, maybe, but she didn't say that. No matter, Winstoke would be there to see her in the beautiful pearls, the ones that came with her family name.

* * *

"Look at that woman over there," one of the ladies in Perry Adler's brother's box said when the lights came up at the first intermission, pointing across the great opera hall auditorium. "She's hung with so many diamonds she looks like the chandelier."

The other women raised their opera glasses or lorgnettes and tittered. Perry's brother identified her as Mrs. Flint, the nabob's widow, and they all laughed at encroaching Cits and Vulgar mushrooms. Everyone except Winstoke, that is, then Perry, when he noticed his friend still staring at the opposite box. "Zeus," he exclaimed, following Winstoke's look, "ain't that Diamond in the box that Belle woman? How did they ever gull a Puritan Cit like the nabob's widow into hosting one of MacDermott's doxies?"

"That *lady*," Winstoke answered through clenched teeth, "is Miss Swann, Lord Harwood's niece, and she would grace any company she chose to keep. Will you excuse me?" And he got up to exit the box, leaving two ruffled doves and an angry matron who'd been hoping to snabble Winstoke for one of her sisters.

"Unmannered brute," she proclaimed.

Perry corrected her: "No, just petticoat fever. Hits a man hard, the first time."

"How would you know, you insensitive clodpoll? I've been throwing girls at you for years now, and you've never dropped the handkerchief."

Perry nodded toward Mrs. Flint's box, where Winstoke was seen bowing over Cristabel's hand. "They never looked like that either."

How different this visit to the opera was from last time. There were no foxed soldiers, no indecent décolletages or indecorous behavior, at least not near Cristabel. Even Major MacDermott was as exquisite in his manners as he was in his kilt, the last of his bruises carefully powdered. Mr. Haynes was as tongue-tied as the two awed spinsters he sat between, so Cristabel was able to enjoy the opera to its fullest, not distracted by anything more than the gleaming prisms cast by Mrs. Flint's dragonhorde of diamonds, and the need, every once in a while, to touch the pearls at her own neck.

That was until the intermission, when he came, filling the box with his elegance, fueling her soul with his smile.

After greetings were exchanged, the others got up to seek refreshment or fresh air. When Cristabel rose to follow, Mrs. Flint gestured her back to her seat. "No, you stay and keep his lordship company. He didn't come to see any of us."

"But I shouldn't—"

"Don't be getting all missish now," the forthright matron ordered. "He ain't going to ravish you, right in view of half the *ton*."

When the box was empty of everyone but the two of them, Winstoke raised her hand to his lips again, sending shivers through her, and smiled. "If it weren't for that bit of lace, I'd be tempted beyond endurance."

She snatched her hand away. "My lord!"

"I'm sorry, Belle. I cannot help teasing you, just to watch you blush. It starts here, and here." He marked the progress with his eyes, but they both knew this was no innocent flirtation.

"How did you like the first act?" she hurriedly interjected, before he could go further, before he could work himself up to the improper offer again.

Winstoke answered impatiently. He didn't *want* to make small talk, but he couldn't find the words. He knew he was off to another bad start—damn, he didn't know this would be so hard. How could he? He'd never proposed before. Hell, he'd never even been in love before. And all those people with their glasses fixed on this box, and her party due back any moment . . .

"Those pearls look lovely on you."

The proposal never came as Cristabel explained how the necklace was part of her uncle's estate and just restored to her. She wanted it made perfectly clear that the pearls were not an ill-gotten gift.

The proposition never came either, to Cristabel's relief. She could not help noticing, however, that Winstoke also never offered to accompany her to the hallway for a walk or a cool drink. Was that what a woman in her position could look forward to? Being kept in the dark, so he needn't embarrass his friends of the *haute monde* by introducing her?

She had to know. "Would you care to walk around a bit before the next act?"

"No, I'd much rather keep you all to myself," he answered, dreading the thought of someone calling him Chase or Captain.

Cristabel fingered those pearls, suddenly as tight as a noose around her neck.

The next act was not quite as enjoyable for Miss Swann. At the break she asked Mac to escort her downstairs, for the air in the box was suffocating her. Coming up the stairs, with a pretty young woman in debutante's white on his arm, was Lord Winstoke. So he could take some society chit out in public, could he, and not her! She turned her own radiant smile on Major MacDermott and laughed up at him. Mac looked stunned—they'd been discussing the dying hero of Act Two—until he noticed the viscount, looking thunderous.

"Oh, no you don't, my girl. I'm not tasting any more of his home-brewed for you, so you can play off your tricks somewhere else." And he turned her around to get back to the box, fast.

Winstoke caught up to them at the top of the stairs, dragging his indignant partner by the arm. "Lady Brandice, may I present Miss Swann, Major MacDermott. Miss Swann, Lady Brandice Westmore. Uh, Lady Brandice expressed a desire for some lemonade, Major. Do you think you might accompany her?"

Accompany her? By Jupiter, he'd accompany Old Nick to hell and back, rather than face this particular devil again. He pulled Lady Brandice back down the stairs.

"That was poorly done, my lord," Cristabel began. "And I doubt Lady Brandice's family will thank you for introducing us."

"What? Oh, MacDermott. The family hasn't a feather to fly with, so there's no worry about fortune hunters like him. He'll lose interest as soon as he hears the size of her dowry. She has three brothers, incidentally. You might mention that to the major."

People were pushing past them now, and he had to speak louder over the noise. "Belle, I don't care about MacDermott or the chit, that's not what I wanted to talk about, but we can't speak here. There is something you have to know, and I swear to tell you tomorrow, if you can just trust me for tonight, no matter what."

"I have something to tell you, too. I realize I have been moralistic and judgmental, especially for one who has no right to cast stones, glass houses and all, but now I am independent, and could not even say circumstances forced me—"

The lights were dimming. He led her back to her box and told her, "Dearest, I have absolutely no idea what you are talking about, but we will straighten it all out tomorrow. Just don't listen to any gossip, and trust me." He quickly kissed her fingers again. "Tomorrow."

Chapter Seventeen

Tomorrow—if she could fall asleep tonight! What with her thoughts in chaos and Meadowlark's snores, Cristabel could not relax. Her emotions had been through the wash-wringer and come out limp and tangled. She'd known the heart-lift of watching his eyes light up when he first saw her, and the agony of the choice. Could she accept a discreet liaison, instead of *carte blanche*, instead of nothing? That way was despair, thinking she might lose his love altogether. She had known jealousy, too, tonight. If she turned green at that insipid deb, heaven knew what she would do if he took a wife. There was satisfaction also, because he was just as jealous over her hand on Mac's arm—she knew he was—and hope, that he asked for her trust. Tomorrow was taking forever to get here.

Cristabel started counting the old dog's breaths as an aid to sleep, but the very irregularity jarred at her consciousness and kept her from slumber. There was a whistling intake, a throat-rattling exhale, with a pause between. Sometimes the breathing out was more like a snort, sometimes the wait between was so long Cristabel wondered if the decrepit animal had breathed her last. The snore would start up again with a huge gasping whoosh—all perfectly audible even with the dog asleep out in Cristabel's tiny sitting room, the bedroom door closed. Meadowlark's bed, that old dress not even a rag-picker would deign to touch now, had been moved to the next room after that debacle in the park, when Cristabel found bread crumbs, a shredded sack, and an ancient, smelly cur, all on *her* bed. Fine watchdog the mongrel was anyway, snarling at Cristabel more often than not for disturbing her cache of bones in Cristabel's closet.

The old mutt was at it again, growling in her dreams at phantom food-snatchers. Now she'd set off the foxhound brought inside to the kitchen at night for the neighbors' sake. Pug would be yapping, Mr. Haynes would be complaining soon—and Mrs. Flint was shrieking!

Cristabel grabbed up her robe and ran through the connecting door, stumbling over Meadowlark, who gnarled at her, and out to the hallway at the top of the stairs. By the light of the candles left burning there, she could see Mrs. Flint, in yards of yellow satin, beating Nick Blass over the head with her reticule.

"Varmint! Sneak thief! A body can't be safe in this sinkhole of a city. Thatchgallows! Attacking an innocent woman in her own bed!"

But he hadn't, Cristabel realized. Nick had attacked the nabob's widow in *Cristabel's* old bed. It was her, not Mrs. Flint at all, that he was after with that wicked-looking knife. It didn't matter to Mrs. Flint, who kept swinging the purse by its strings at the dastard's head and screaming, or to Pug, who was bouncing around in a wheezing frenzy.

Nick sliced through the reticule's ties and ran toward the backstairs, until he saw Fanny and Boy brandishing pots and pans and the howling foxhound scrabbling down the corridor. He raced to the front, where Mrs. Flint was joined by Mac, bony ankles sticking out of a yellow satin robe with a feather boa, fire poker in his hand.

"You'll hang for this, you maw-worm!" he shouted over all the commotion, but he was careful to stay shielded behind Mrs. Flint's bulk in the doorway of her room. *Not* the stairs from his room, Cristabel noted.

Two heads in identical, frilled nightcaps were peeking around an upstairs door exclaiming "Dear, dear!" and Mr. Haynes was starting an angry march down the stairs, while Cristabel stood frozen at the landing. Then Marie came out of her door, wanting to know what was happening.

Nick looked up at the sound and saw his nemesis. "You!" he spat out and rushed at Cristabel up the stairs, waving the knife.

There was no place for her to go, no handy vase to throw or chair to hide behind; there was only that knife. And the screaming from below.

"You jade, you! You started this whole bloody mess with your fine airs 'n innocent blushes. Hah! Innocent be damned. You wanted my share, is all! I've seen you carryin' on with your fine lord, just like any other whore—"

"Don't you talk to me like that, you wretched runt. It wasn't me who made a living off women and terrorized them with vile threats. *I* didn't rob and cheat and lie!"

"Doxie! I'll have your kidneys carved up for the dogs! I'll—"

"You'll be hanged for sure, you misbegotten dwarf! Look at all the witnesses, fool. You'll never get away with this!"

He snarled. "It's too late. At least I'll have my revenge!" And he leaped at her again. Lights glinted off the steel blade and off the maniac glow in his eyes. Cristabel darted to the side. Marie shrieked. Mr. Haynes tossed his slippers down at Nick's head and missed, and the tableau downstairs was frozen. Except for Pug.

Meadowlark had wandered out of Cristabel's rooms to see what the commotion was, mainly concerned if the banging of pots and pans meant a chance of another meal. Nothing smelled like food, so the old dog collapsed in a distempered heap in the hallway. She did snap at Nick's shoe when he brushed past her, just because she had been disturbed for no good reason. She got up growling and moved to a less trafficked area at the top of the stairs.

Now Pug may have gone into an asthmatic fit at the attack on his mistress, and he may almost have passed out from lack of air, yipping so long and hard, but this was serious business. No one threatened his Meadowlark without suffering the consequences. Those little legs trundled that squat body up the stairs in a blur, and those baby bulldog jaws opened as wide as they could and clamped down on the back of Nick Blass's ankle, hard. Pop-eyes bulging even more, the little gladiator hung on and on, despite Nick's shouts and foot-shakings. Nick flicked the knife aside bare inches from Cristabel's throat, turning to make mincemeat out of Pug.

Cristabel screamed "Mac!" and looked past Nick's shoulder, to distract him. Mac collapsed in a dead faint at Mrs. Flint's feet, but Nick did turn around. Cristabel gave his back a shove and he stumbled forward, Pug still keeping him off balance. He tripped over Meadowlark and went tumbling down the stairs.

Cristabel darted back to her room for the forgotten pistol and returned, crying, "Stop it! Stop it, all of you!" as she raced down the stairs to where Fanny and Boy were beating Nick about the head with their skillets, and Mrs. Flint had emptied the elephant-foot umbrella stand and was jabbing him in the ribs with a lace parasol. Mrs. Todd was clutching her husband and sobbing, and Mac was now casting up his accounts. Mrs. Flint's servants were peering over the bannisters; they disappeared when Cristabel waved the gun in their direction.

Nick was not a pretty sight when everyone stood back. The erstwhile bully was now a broken man, at least one arm's worth. His good hand held the piece of his ear cut off by his own knife, which Cristabel picked up at arm's length and handed to Mr. Haynes, who blanched as if she'd handed him a snake. Pug was still shredding Nick's pant leg, while the foxhound was licking the tears streaming down his cheeks. Blass looked up into the not-quite steady barrel of Cristabel's pistol.

"That's it," he wept. "I lived by women, now I guess I'll die by a woman. Dust to dust. I were never much, chaps always laughed at me. Now they're gonna laugh at me bein' shot by a skirt."

"I doubt they do much laughing where you're going," Cristabel told him dryly.

"Then do it, if you're gonna. Put me out of my misery. Short people never get any breaks."

It was Mrs. Flint, Pug now clamped to her ample bosom where he was starting to wheeze again from lack of air, who asked if Cristabel knew how to use the pistol she was wielding, or should they call the watch.

"I shot a tree once," Cristabel assured her. "But you needn't worry about my aim. The gun is not loaded."

Nick looked disgusted and sat up straighter, holding a dirty kerchief to his ear, eyeing the distance to the front door. Boy moved to block his escape, and he hunched over again, blubbering in misery.

"Sure, call the charlie. I got nowhere to run. I been sleepin' in alleys with the garbage rats. Prison's at least a roof over my head."

"I should think attempted murder is a hanging offense, or at least deportation, to say nothing of breaking and entering."

"What was I to do? I don't know no other trade 'n the girls 'as all gone respectable or to respectable 'ouses. Now it's the devil's necktie for old Nick Blass, that or end a slave in Botany Bay. Mac, too, likely."

Cristabel and Mrs. Flint chorused: "Mac, too?"

"You don't expect me to go by myself, do you?"

Cristabel could just see it: the magistrate's hearing, the witnesses Gwen and Alice and Kitty, the house, the whole sordid mess out in the open, with Major MacDermott's name in the papers and cartoons, right under hers!

"I didn't know! I didn't know!" Mac was crying, on his knees in Mrs. Flint's bathrobe. It was that lady's beseeching look which finally decided Miss Swann. The scandal would touch her, and everyone in the house. And Mrs. Flint really cared for Mac, as seemed obvious from his choice of bedchambers . . .

"Would you rather go in the Navy? I cannot let you run loose in London, Nick. You know that. And I have no call to be lenient with you after what you've tried to do. So that's the choice: I call the watch, or you take the King's shilling and get out of my life."

"But we're at war!"

"That's the only reason they would take a sorry specimen such as you. Well?"

"The nubbing cheat or the Navy? I knew you were a hard woman the minute you wanted me to wear a bloody uniform. Looks like you'll get your wish after all."

Cristabel directed Fanny and Boy to tie Nick up and lock him in the storeroom, and keep watch. She asked Mr. Haynes to watch *them*, intending to hand him the gun.

"Oh no, I couldn't. I have to go write this up for the *Chronicle*. Mr. Helfhopher will love it. Action, danger, virtue triumphant, even mercy. He'll have to give me that promotion, an increase, a better desk—"

"Mr. Haynes."

"Yes, Miss Swann?" he said, halfway up the stairs.

"I believe you heard me say this pistol is not now loaded?"

"Yes, yes, I have to remember to put that in."

"Mr. Haynes, I have the ammunition for the gun right here in the pocket of my robe. Remember this when you even think about mentioning any of the events of this evening to your Mr. Helfhopher or anyone else: I have never missed what I have aimed at. Have I made myself clear?"

"I cannot write anything, not even if I change the names?"

"You do and you won't need a new desk."

He gulped. "What was it you wished me to do?"

Cristabel went upstairs to dress, searching for something suitable for a respectable single lady to wear to pay a call on an unrelated bachelor in the middle of the night. If there were such a thing. She found the last of her schoolmistress dresses, the gray merino that hadn't been cut up for uniforms or rags or used as a dog's bed. It buttoned to the collar and the cuffs, but with her filled-out form, it did not look like a sack anymore; with the paisley shawl it would serve the purpose.

Marie came in from administering laudanum to the Douglas sisters and shook her head. "You look like you're dressing for the magistrate's. I thought you were sending for Lord Winstoke. He would be a lot likelier to do what you want if you looked a little more helpless, or haven't you learned anything?"

"I am not sending for anyone. It's too complicated to put in a letter, and what if he wasn't home, or the servants didn't waken him? Furthermore, it's Captain Chase I am going to for help. He would know a lot more about enlisting someone in the Navy, and he offered to stand my friend any number of times."

"The captain, hm? In that case I better go with you." Marie scampered away to dress. Cristabel was certain Marie would not look like a dowdy parishioner, not if she thought Jonas Sparling might see her. She was also sure Marie would not have insisted on accompanying her, if her destination had been Winstoke's lodgings.

That was another reason she would not ask the viscount for help: she didn't know where he lived. She knew all about the family property in Staffordshire, but he only mentioned a temporary place in Mayfair. Maybe he was staying with friends. No matter, she did not want him hearing the filth Nick Blass could spew in his anger, not when she was trying to convince his lordship of her respectability. Captain Chase would not think the less of her, no matter what lies the guttersnipe made up. And if he did, so what?

If the captain was not at home, if, heaven forbid, he was "entertaining" again, then she would have no recourse but to go to Winstoke with the whole sorry, disgraceful mess, unless she wanted the affair made public. She had no doubt that a hackney driver could find the location of one of London's premier lords, even if he had gone on to some elegant ball after the opera or one of his clubs. The idea of the viscount entertaining in Captain Chase's fashion was too abhorrent to consider. Cristabel firmly pinned her hair into a no-nonsense bun and called Marie.

Mac was dressed, and flourishing his sword downstairs in the parlor. He hurried to find her a hackney, relieved she had not asked him to accompany her. "That fellow don't like me above half," he explained, touching his eye.

"I thought it was Winstoke who you ah, disliked." She nearly said "feared" but amended that, for his pride's sake.

"Yeah, him, too."

Chapter Eighteen

The same door knocker, with the Harwood family crest nearby. The same interminable wait. The same knock-in-the-cradle footman.

Adam's apple bulging, nightcap falling over his eyes, Floyd opened the door, saw Miss Swann, said, "Oh no, not you again," and slammed the door in her face.

Cristabel rapped again, louder. The door opened immediately this time. "Hush up, do," Floyd begged. "You'll wake his lordship and he'll have my hide, he will. Criminy, what a woman for mingle-mangles!"

"Nonsense. I need to see Captain Chase immediately, and he will be extremely displeased if you don't fetch him. He is not, ah, occupied, is he?"

Now Floyd grinned insolently. "Tucked up tight in his own bed. Want to go see?"

Cristabel colored, but stood her ground. "I cannot imagine Captain Chase being pleased that his friends are insulted on his doorstep. I hope you can swim."

Friends, were they? Floyd gulped. She was looking better than last time, and he was getting fond of this place. "I'll go get the master, miss. Right away. Would you care to wait in the sitting room?"

Marie called after him, "Find Mr. Sparling, too, while you're at it."

*   *   *

Someone came to light the fire, and someone else brought a tea tray. Marie disappeared, and Cristabel paced. She knew if she sat on that sofa near where the captain and the redhead had . . . she'd have a fit of the giggles, that's what. She laughed softly, until she remembered the man's awful temper and bellowing rage. Maybe it was a mistake to come here after all. Maybe she should have searched out Lord Winstoke . . .

"Belle, what are you doing here?"

Belle? Winstoke? "My lord, what are you doing here?"

The viscount's mouth quirked. This was where the whole thing had started. "This is, ah, where I have been staying in the city."

"Then you and Captain Chase know each other?" Cristabel was dismayed that they had discussed her.

Winstoke hesitated a moment, then told her, "Yes, we are friends. Usually." The ludicrousness of the situation brought out the devilry in him and he could not resist teasing: "You haven't come for an assignation with him, have you?"

"Don't be goosish. I hardly know the man."

"Good. I would hate to have to call the bounder out. I daresay his *cherie amie* wouldn't dress like a Sunday school teacher anyway."

"Do be serious, my lord."

"But I am. You look different." So different, in fact, that no one but a blind man could have mistaken her for a member of the muslin company. Blast!

He looked different, too. With his shirt unbuttoned at the collar and untucked in his breeches, his jacket slung over one shoulder and his hair still sleep-tousled, falling in curls, he looked like a swashbuckling pirate, right down to the gleam in his eye and the mischief in his smile. At the very least he looked precisely like the darkly handsome hero of one of Maria Edgeworth's romances, ready to ride *ventre à terre* to the heroine's rescue. Except, of course, that he was no horseman. She was no heroine either, and her heart would *not* pound in her chest at the sight of him, or her breathing come fast and short. She turned away.

"Please, I need to see Captain Chase." Rats, she was panting!

"I'm sorry, Belle. I know you wouldn't have come here if it weren't important. Chase is, um, out of town. Let me help, please."

So she started to tell him, but she did not get far.

"Someone tried to kill you? I'll see him dead!" Now there was murder in those gray eyes, and his mouth was thinned to a harsh line. "Are you all right?" He grabbed her shoulders and shook her, staring into her eyes for the answer, then pulled her into his arms for quick reassurance. Cristabel struggled and he released her immediately. "I am sorry, my dear. You really are all right?"

"I was," she said breathlessly, and proceeded to finish her story, taking pleasure in watching the emotions flicker across his chiseled features from anger and horror to amusement and pride.

"You really pointed an unarmed pistol at the skirter?"

She left out nothing, not the dogs nor the frying pans, nor Nick's threats, no matter how embarrassing. "I did not want you to hear his foul ravings," she said, looking away.

"What, did you fear I would believe such bilge water—such muck?" He gently touched her shoulder, turning her to face him. "I thought I told you to trust me."

"Yes, but—"

"Sh," placing a finger on her lips. "Let us take care of

first things first. What did you want me—Chase—to do about this Blass scum?"

"I do not want him murdered in my house," she answered sternly, and he smiled and promised.

"I thought that sending him to the Navy would be the best solution. He would not have a chance to air his lies or be a threat. And I would not have his soul on my conscience."

"I have never thought much of the practice of having criminals serve aboard ships. They don't make any better sailors than they made honest citizens, but I agree: having the man stand for trial would only air a lot of dirty linen."

"Then do you think I should contact Captain Chase to make the arrangements? I cannot very well keep the man incarcerated in my storeroom forever."

"I can take care of everything for you, never fear. There's a cutter at the docks right now that could see him on the way to Bristol at daybreak. I'll take care of it this instant."

"I seem to be in your debt again. I don't know how—"

"Wait here, that's how."

"Oh, but I couldn't."

"Please. I don't want you to have to see that makebait again. And we have so much to discuss. It's almost tomorrow anyway, and I promised an explanation. You'll be safe here, and I won't have to worry. Please, Belle?"

She had already entered a bachelor's house after dark, so she couldn't be more compromised, especially not after living in that house in Kensington. And there was the promised explanation, the one that seemed tied to laughing eyes and a tender smile she could not resist. She nodded.

"Good, good. Ring for whatever you need, and the library is right through there if you wish to find a book or newspaper. Make yourself at home. . . . I suppose that sounds peculiar, since this was once your family home."

"Oh, no, I never lived here."

"No?" he asked thoughtfully. "The place suits you, quiet and refined, yet comfortable, too."

"Thank you. I am sure Captain Chase is content."

"Is he? . . . I better be off." He held her hand an instant, then brought it to his mouth. He turned her hand over and kissed the inside of her wrist. "I'll be back as soon as possible."

He did not go out toward the hallway but went through to the library instead, leaving the door open. Cristabel could see him open a drawer in the desk and remove a pistol.

She moved to the doorway and watched him load the weapon, then place it in the waistband of his pants.

"You won't do anything rash?"

"I promised, didn't I?"

"And you will be very, very careful and come back to me soon?"

"Trust me, sweetheart."

She had heard *that* before! She stood next to Uncle Charles's desk. Captain Chase's desk, where he had sat that dreadful day with the lawyers. There was even a ship model in a bottle on top of some papers. She touched the replica idly, listening to the commotion in the hall as his lordship called for a carriage and Jonas Sparling. It was natural, she assumed, for him to draft the captain's man for such a mission.

Then she heard someone bellowing: "Heave to, you scurvy sea-snail. Pipe the mizzen, we sail with the wind."

"Aye-aye, Cap'n."

And she had heard that before, too! Cristabel sank down into the big leather chair behind the desk.

Oh Lord.

The ship, the house. Her house in Kensington. Trust him?

Oh no, she groaned again, she couldn't have been that stupid, could she? Had her brains been changed to sawdust, that she could not tell she had been the butt of a cruel joke? No, no, and no! He could not have known her identity the whole time; he was not simply playing games. Chase had been bandaged, that was a given. He didn't recognize her any better than she knew him that day in the park when Mac introduced them. Mac! He must have known all along. That black eye was nothing compared to what she would do to him. And here she was trying to protect his good name!

So many things fell into place: Mac's innuendoes, the war years Winstoke never wanted to talk about, that scar half-hidden by his long hair. Sparling had told her all about the injury and the loss of his ship. Of course he was no expert with horses, after all those years at sea, or proficient at recognizing ladies. No, he knew all about every type of woman. It was Cristabel's own circumstances that led to the confusion.

When had Winstoke—Chase—discovered her identity? When he stopped calling her Belle and making improper advances, that's when. When the kind letters from the captain started coming, and Jonas Sparling started hanging about the house in Kensington. Winstoke had to have realized well before this evening that she was still unaware of his names and titles. Telling her that Chase was a friend of his, indeed! Of course, she reminded herself, there were all those explanations he was going to make.

What a ninny he must think her. At least one thing was clear: whatever else he may think of her, he knew she was a lady. She moved the ship model closer, and saw that it rested on a lace-edged handkerchief, her handkerchief, that she thought she'd lost at the opera last night. Was it just last night? A smile came to her lips. She thought she might trust him, after all.

When he got back, she was sitting quietly at his desk, *Invicta* in her hands. A good sign, he thought, *Invicta* was still in one piece. He had realized the library held too many clues, and it was just a matter of time, but it was past time, and now that she had a chance to get used to the idea . . .

"Who are you?" Her voice was steady, but he could see the confusion, hurt, and anger in her eyes, mingled with something else, hope, perhaps.

"I am Kenley Chase, Viscount Winstoke, London's greatest jackass, and the man who loves you. But who are you? One minute you are a goddess, come to tempt mortal man, the next you are an avenging Fury, sent to keep him on the straight and narrow."

"I am only the vicar's daughter who believes in Father Christmas, a naive school teacher who knows less about the world than any of her students, and Miss Cristabel Swann, who tries to run a respectable boardinghouse. And—" She couldn't say it.

"And not my Belle?"

"Oh Lee, I shouldn't, I swore I couldn't, but I fear I would be, for you!"

His arms were open and she was in them, fitting as naturally as sunlight to the rose.

"And I would marry you even if you were the wash maid scrubbing the stairs."

"Marry? Did you really say marry?"

"Of course, you silly goose, how else could I have you in my arms and by my side, forever? Besides, I promised Fanny to make an honest woman out of you."

"Oh, I forgot about Fanny and Boy guarding Nick, and all the rest. Is everything all right?"

"It is now," he said, kissing the top of her head and stepping back. "But come, let us go sit in the parlor. With the doors open, of course! We have a great deal to discuss and I don't want the servants gossiping, and quite frankly, I have waited so long to make you mine I hardly trust myself."

"Marie is somewhere about. She can chaperone." If there was a tinge of regret in Cristabel's voice, it was hidden in his laughter.

"Marie went with Sparling, off on an errand. I'm afraid your companion does not set a good example. But come."

Why he thought the parlor was more respectable than the library when he was the one—"What about the red-head?" she asked as soon as they were seated in facing chairs. She did not care right then if Nick Blass was sent to Bristol or Baluchistan.

"What redhead?" He followed her gaze to the rug by the fireplace, and crooked the corners of his mouth up in that way she adored. "Don't you know that I have not had eyes for anyone but you since the bandages came off?"

"Ah. And here I was on my way to being infatuated with Captain Chase."

"What, that paltry fellow? I thought you considered him a thief, a liar, and a rakehell."

"Don't remind me. I said so many outrageous things that I had no business saying to anyone!"

"We made a rare mull of it, didn't we? You do understand that I never knew about the house in Kensington when I sent you there, don't you? And then, when I knew about that house, I didn't know it was you?"

She chuckled delightedly at his muddled speech and told him it no longer mattered.

"But it must," he said, coming to sit on the floor by her chair, holding her hand. "You have not told me that you love me."

"I must have loved you forever, even when I was furious at you, or when I was trying to convince myself not to, for you could never love me. But that day in the park when you were nearly killed by the horses, I nearly died, too, thinking I had lost you."

"And I ached for fear you had come to harm through my foolish pride. That would have been worse than the *Invicta,* and I could not have borne it."

"I don't understand. Sparling said you were magnificent on the ship, that the men worshiped you."

He stared at the fire. "And they are all dead. I could have run, instead of standing to fight against the odds."

"But that's bravery, not pride. I'm sure your men would not have wanted it any other way. I would not want to change you." She squeezed his hand, and he returned a brilliant smile.

"Then what a favor Blass did us! It was he, you know, who fired the shot that frightened the horses in the first place. That matter is all taken care of, incidentally. Blass is on his way and shall likely be convinced to jump ship in the Americas or somewhere equally distant. He will never bother you again."

"That's perfect. Now Mac doesn't have to worry about news of his activities getting back to his commander either, and he can rejoin his regiment."

"I have a feeling the major will be marching to Mrs. Flint's drum soon enough. Imagine the *ton*'s reaction: the nabob's widow and the black sheep."

"Will they be cut, do you think?"

"I doubt they'd care. If so, a viscountess surely has enough social standing to see them through."

"Oh. My lord—"

"Kenley."

She took her hands from under his and twisted them in her lap. "You do not have to marry me, my—Kenley."

"I like the sound of that, 'my Kenley.' And I do not *have* to do anything but make you happy. But what bee have you got in your bonnet now, my Bluebell?"

"I . . . I had almost decided to come to you anyway, with no strings. That's the real test, according to Marie."

"Then why is my man Sparling giving in his notice to go into the dressmaking business?"

"Is he? How wonderful!"

"Yes, a one-handed valet was something of a challenge. But still, madam, that does not excuse the slur to my sons' honor. You cannot expect them to be always defending their parentage, can you? Furthermore, your little Fanny has her heart set on being lady's maid to a 'genuine' lady, and my mother is looking to spoil her grandchildren unmercifully. You wouldn't disappoint them all, would you, or me, an old sea dog who hopes to give up his rakehell ways and become a country gentleman, enjoying hearth and home and the love of a very, very good woman?"

"But I have no dowry."

"Good, then no one will accuse me of being a fortune hunter. You do have a dowry, however: that very troublesome house on Sullivan Street and a very fine set of pearls."

"The pearls! Kenley, were they really a Harwood inheritance?"

He stood and went into the library, where Cristabel could hear him opening drawers in the desk. Coming back, he held out a velvet-covered box. "Of course those

were Harwood jewels. Here are the Winstoke engage-
ment emeralds. Will you wear them, Cristabel, my love?"

For answer she stepped into his embrace and their kiss
was a promise.

Sometime later, not even a short time later, as these
things are measured, when the pins were out of Cristabel's hair and her dress was not so securely fastened, they
broke apart at a cough. The footman Floyd entered the
room with a tea tray.

"Who the deuce ordered tea at a time like this?" Winstoke demanded, while Cristabel turned her glowing face
away.

"Mrs. Witt, the housekeeper, my lord, she insisted."
Floyd's voice was shaky and the tea things rattled in his
unsteady grip. He put the tray down and fled.

"I think I had better go home, Kenley," Cristabel said
when they were once more alone, before she could answer the yearning in his eyes with her own heart's
hunger.

"You are home, my dear, right here at Harwood
House."

"But I couldn't . . . we can't . . ."

"Yes, we can, as soon as Sparling and Marie return
with the special license and your clothes. Then we can
travel together to Staffordshire without offending anyone's sensibilities, where I am certain my mother will
plan a wedding breakfast for the whole county. We are
going to do it up right, my prim and proper lady, with no
more cupboard kisses."

. . . Except maybe a few before the vicar comes.

⦰ SIGNET

Lords & Ladies from Signet

HISTORICAL ROMANCE